THE VIKING SANDS: ENDGAME

a sequel to

The Viking Sands

Thomas Torrens

The Viking Sands: Endgame, Copyright © 2022 by Thomas Torrens.

All rights reserved. No part of this book may be reproduced or transmitted in any form or by any means without written permission of the author.

Please contact the author with your comments and feedback at: thomastorrens@aol.com

Dedicated to my two loving daughters,
Gina and Laura,
And with very special thanks to my best friend, Ian.

AUTHOR'S NOTE: *This new thriller is a sequel to The Viking Sands, published in 2011. You could read this book without having read its predecessor, but much would be missed in context, clarity and continuity. I have attempted from the outset to bring the reader quickly into the picture from where the original novel left off, but I strongly recommend that you should read it first to enjoy the full knowledge and experience of this fast-moving duology of thrillers.*

CONTENTS

Prologue ix
Part 1 Resurrection 1
Part 2 The Double-Headed Eagle 25
Part 3 Sabotage and War Clouds 47
Part 4 Clarity and the Cosmos 67
Part 5 The Saudi Apocalypse 85
Part 6 The US Strategic Petroleum Reserve 97
Part 7 The Middle Kingdom 109
Part 8 Redemption and Revenge 127
Part 9 Endgame 153
Epilogue 169

PROLOGUE

"Choose your friends carefully. Your enemies will choose you."

I

Thursday, March, 7th, Intermediate Oil Pipeline Pumping Station at the Crude Oil Processing Plant, Abqaiq, Eastern Province, Saudi Arabia, 05:00 GMT +2

Essam al-Hamzah was getting increasingly nervous. Somehow Saudi Aramco's Chief Operations Superintendent sensed that it was going to be a very bad day. The 'Smart PIG' cleaning device that was scheduled to arrive through the pipeline from the Ras Tanura seaport was already half an hour late. Considering the massive volumes of crude oil that were moved daily from the supergiant Ghawar oilfield through the Abqaiq processing plant to Saudi Arabia's principal marine export terminal at Ras Tanura on the Persian Gulf, every second lost was critical. Although the sun wouldn't rise yet for several hours producing its scorching daily heat, al-Hamzah could feel a cold bead of sweat trickle uncomfortably down the back of his neck. He knew well that time was money and that any time lost from the already tight daily oil transportation schedule was unforgivable.

"Sherif," he barked at his assistant, "check the telemetry readout on the pipeline. What's delaying the incoming PIG?"

"It doesn't say, sir. I'll call them immediately at Ras Tanura to find out."

PIGs (Pipeline Inspection Gauges) are sent as heavy, tight fitting, high-pressure driven projectiles traveling through pipelines at 7 meters/second (25.2 km/hour) to perform routine maintenance operations without interrupting the flow of oil in the line behind them. They are used primarily to clean the pipes, but 'Smart PIGs' can also perform advanced ultrasound inspection activities to measure any corrosion, metal loss, pitting, weld anomalies and/or cracking damage to pipelines. Regular pigging of the pipelines was essential to maintain a smooth flow of crude oil from the wellheads in the vast 59 billion barrel Ghawar oilfield complex, through Abqaiq, to the tanker-loading flanges at the Saudi's maritime export terminal on the Gulf.

Two minutes later Sherif returned with an update. "It seems that the PIG had to be fitted first with some special new SCADA (Supervisory Control and Data Acquisition) telemetry equipment, sir. Some German engineers were flown in from Lingen to install and test it. But it's all done now and the PIG should be arriving momentarily."

"Finally!" al-Hamzah thought. He couldn't afford any further slippage in the day's precise schedule.

Green lights flashed and bells rang repeatedly to announce the arrival of the incoming PIG from Ras Tanura. The pipeline had been successfully cleansed back to there. Now it only needed to be further cleaned up to the feeder flanges that were connected to the northern end of the sprawling Ghawar oilfield, located some 62 kilometers down the line. There the 36" pipeline would receive the first of the day's numerous batches of oil destined initially for treatment in the Abqaiq crude oil processing facility.

After a brief and cursory inspection by X-ray, the PIG was sent speedily on its way for its remaining journey to the Ghawar terminal, just over 2 hours away, at the southwest end of the pipeline. Al-Hamzah finally breathed a sigh of relief as he threw the switch to dispatch it. "Perhaps," he thought, "this won't be such a bad day after all."

THE VIKING SANDS : ENDGAME

II

Thursday, March 7th, Dhahran Aramco Compound, Eastern Province, Saudi Arabia, 07:10 GMT +2

Sixty nine kilometers to the northeast, in the former expatriate community of Dhahran, Jack Samson was up early as usual. He wanted to complete his daily 8 kilometer morning run before the unbearable heat of the day arrived shortly after sunrise. Samson was a communications specialist who had just been seconded to Saudi Aramco by Chevron, one of its former owners. He would soon be busy assisting their Saudi staff in operating their new state-of-the art SCADA telemetry system. The system would monitor and control the daily transport of almost 4 million barrels a day (bbls/day) of crude oil through the intricate web of gathering, feeder and main trunk lines from the huge Ghawar oilfield, first to Abqaiq for processing, and then on to both the VLCC and ULCC tankers waiting to be loaded at the Ras Tanura maritime export terminal.

As Samson started his circuit of the compound the eastern horizon had begun to glow a warm pink from the rays of the soon to rise morning sun. The late winter constellations overhead grew dim in the diffuse, pre-dawn light. It looked like it would be another hot and humid day in the Gulf region.

To the west the sky was still dark with the remnants of the quickly vanishing night. Samson breathed in the cool morning air and relentlessly upped his pace. But suddenly everything changed dramatically! Without any warning an ear-splitting explosion emanated from the southwest, followed instantly by a series of billowing fireballs rolling outwards along the far horizon. They soon paled in comparison to the immense blue-white aura that quickly followed, erupting high into the distant sky and turning the early dawn into instant midday. Crackling with searing heat and static electricity, the monstrous tempest emanated precisely from the direction of the Ghawar oilfield, preceded by a massive shock wave that was leveling all before it as it went.

Samson was stunned by what he saw unfolding in the far distance. But it was, nonetheless, eerily familiar as well. His last assignment had been at Chevron's office in Aberdeen, Scotland, at the time when the cataclysmic Sterling Oilfield disaster had occurred, offshore in the North Sea. He had seen first-hand those remaining members of the shell-shocked crew of the Sterling platform disembark from their incoming helicopter in a dazed and disoriented state. He had both watched videos of and been told in detail of the dreaded, dazzling blue-white aura that had signaled the complete destruction of an entire oilfield. And now, unbelievably, it seemed to be happening again! This sudden occurrence was completely unexpected. Yet Samson could not deny the horrifically familiar sight he was seeing unfold right there before his very eyes....

PART 1
RESURRECTION

"Every blizzard starts with a few gentle snowflakes."

I

Five months earlier on Wednesday, October 24th, Cerro Torre Glacier, Argentine Patagonia, 07:00 GMT

"Cold, cold, bitter cold; dark as a tomb." were the first dim thoughts of a now barely conscious Albert Stern. But to his utter disbelief he was still alive, although deeply entombed in a smothering cocoon of powder snow, piled in high drifts at the foot of Cerro Torre's sheer east face, from which he had fallen an indeterminate time before.

As he had fallen from the precipitous heights above, a peculiarly Patagonian upward-swirling wind from the east of over 70 mph had buoyed him up like a dancing kite. But he had blacked out almost immediately, resigning himself to his cruel and inevitable fate.

Fortuitously, an unseasonal spring blizzard the night before had dumped almost 2 meters of fresh powder on the usually wind-scoured Torre Glacier. It had cushioned his landing, although now he was nearly suffocating from the swirling spindrift clogging his nose, throat and air passages. He struggled mightily to free himself and reach upwards for the safety of the sunlight and fresh air above him.

The chances of his having survived such a fall from the heights of the vertical granite needle above him were infinitesimal. Yet as he gingerly moved his arms and legs Albert realized that he had beaten all the odds against his survival. His growing consciousness struggled with this fact.

Finally able to emerge from his frozen chrysalis, he stood chest deep in the cumulous powder and drank in the warmth of the fickle Patagonian sun. No one would ever believe that he was still alive!

But Albert was struggling to put himself into context. He was 40 years old; tall and handsomely slim; muscular, with a Semitic olive complexion; wavy dark hair; intense brown eyes; and normally in possession of an acute memory. Inexplicably, though, there seemed to be a deep, blank void in what was usually his memory's unlimited recall capacity. All that registered in his addled brain was that he was Alberto Portillo Lopez, the *patron* of *Estancia Huemul*, set solitarily on the outskirts of the helter-skelter climbers' paradise of El Chalten. He knew that he had come to this desolate spot with a guide the day before to climb the 3,128 meter granite dagger of Cerro Torre. He could vividly remember the horror of falling off its vertical rock face. But that was all he knew. Desperately tired and fatigued, he couldn't even start to recall anything of his life before the events of the last day. Only vague and tantalizing shadows of things past flickered fleetingly through his subconscious. Some form of temporary amnesia from his near death experience, he thought? Surely, he hoped, it would soon pass. For now all he could manage was to reflect long and hard on what had actually happened to him. Had his fall really been just an unfortunate climbing accident? What of the unusual sharp report he thought he had heard just as the rope was breaking? It had certainly sounded like a gunshot to him. Why though? Who would want to kill him?

Massively confused, ridden with aches and pains and still quite dazed, Albert knew only that he, Lopez, had to find his way back immediately to his *estancia* where he could quietly collect his thoughts; try to make sense of what had just happened to him; and see if he could puzzle out what would be its likely consequences.

II

Friday, October 26th, CIA Headquarters, Langley, Virginia, 09:30 EDT

Chris Wytham, head of the CIA's Counter-Terrorism Unit, sat before his cluttered desk and looked pensively out the window at the riot of autumn colored leaves falling gracefully into the courtyard below. His prolonged stay in Argentine Patagonia covertly to sanction Albert Stern had taken quite a toll on both his accumulating workload and his personal life. But that was normal for those in his chosen profession.

Wytham was in his early 50s. Tall and wiry, he looked younger than his age. He had handsomely chiseled facial features and dark, curly hair, not yet showing any signs of gray. His penetrating blue eyes radiated a simmering intensity, softened only by an incongruous pair of rimless wire glasses. He had been with the Agency for over 25 years. His postings had included Chief of Station positions in US embassies in Amman, Jakarta, Moscow and Nairobi.

Involved for most of his career in covert operations, he was the CIA's acknowledged expert in profiling the minds of terrorists. He was also amongst the best of the Agency's senior operatives who specialized in remorselessly hunting down and eliminating them. A veteran of many clandestine rendition missions in far-off places in the world, he had successfully caught; brutally interrogated; and permanently incarcerated terrorists on behalf of the US government and its allies over the many years.

Turning to the most immediate matter at hand, he hastened to put the final touches on his Argentine Trip Report:

THOMAS TORRENS

"TOP SECRET Eyes Only
MEMORANDUM FOR: Tim Baker, Director, Central Intelligence Agency
FROM: Chris Wytham, Director, Counter-Terrorism Unit
COPY TO: C-TU Team Members
SUBJECT: Sanction of Albert Stern; Disposition of the Viking Sands

I. Factual Background
Following numerous successful orbital and surface exploration missions to Mars, it was decided to send a second generation of Viking missions there, finally to collect representative soil samples (the Viking Sands – referred to herein as "VS") and to bring them back to Earth for testing in a sterile and secure receiving lab at NASA's HQs in Houston. This was accomplished by the return to Earth of the Viking 3 spacecraft with a suitable quantity of Martian soil. During the first phase of the testing an unexpected explosion occurred in the lab that later proved to be the result of a violent reaction between the VS and a test sample of crude oil. Further forensic examination established without doubt that either a biochemical or biological agent contained in the VS soil appeared to have an explosive and insatiable appetite for both crude oil and its refined products. In the wrong hands, the VS could thus be the ultimate weapon of the 21st century.

NASA's Senior Project Director, Albert Stern, was charged with overseeing exhaustive tests on the VS. But after the explosion in the lab in Houston occurred, both he and the remaining VS disappeared. We now know that he fled first to London and then on to Scotland, at a time that coincided with the catastrophic destruction of the vast UK Sterling oilfield in the North Sea. We traced him subsequently to Geneva, Chamonix, Amsterdam, Buenos Aires and ultimately to Argentine Patagonia, where I was tasked with the duty finally to sanction him with extreme prejudice. It will be recalled that the VS have almost limitless destructive power. We also know now that Stern is a known sociopath who feels no guilt for the consequences of his acts. He used the VS both to eliminate the UK's giant Sterling oilfield and subsequently to consume all of Iran's proved oil reserves, triggering a cataclysmic nuclear exchange between Iran and Israel. In time, it appeared that all remaining traces on Earth of the VS were totally used up or destroyed, but this still cannot be definitively confirmed. However, it is forbidden to obtain any additional soil samples by mandate of a UN Security Council Resolution banning indefinitely all interplanetary flights to Mars. This very specific Resolution overrides the provisions of the Outer Space Treaty of 1967 prohibiting the placing of offensive weapons into Earth's orbit. Indeed, it charges the US government strictly to enforce the ban with its orbital laser cannons, aimed to interdict any such attempted Martian missions by any country.

II. Unresolved issues

Pursuant to your instructions to carry out the President's direct sanction order, I tracked Stern to the town of El Chalten in Argentine Patagonia. He was living there as a wealthy recluse in an old *estancia* on the edge of town on the bribery money that he had been paid by the Israelis in their futile attempt to acquire the VS. Knowing of his great affinity for mountaineering, I waited patiently for him to attempt a climb of the treacherous granite spire, Cerro Torre. Hidden in a sniper's nest on a col below, I watched him while he climbed its sheer east wall with his local guide. From there I witnessed an accident, precipitated in part by my rifle shot aimed at the piton anchor from which he was being belayed. The anchor dislodged and the belay rope frayed and snapped. I clearly saw him begin to plummet down the face in a fall that no one would expect him possibly to have survived. However, due to the combination of high winds blowing sudden and heavy horizontal snowfall and dense fog intermittently obscuring my view, I never saw him actually hit the glacier at the foot of the wall. Nor has his body ever been recovered by either Argentine local or Federal authorities, despite their numerous, exhaustive searches. Thus, improbable as it may seem, there remains the scant possibility that Stern survived the fall and is still alive. If such is true, he could represent an ongoing danger to our national security and to that of the rest of the world.

Equally, while we know that the majority of the remaining VS were destroyed by drone fire when Stern went to retrieve them from the cache he had made for them in the French Alps above Chamonix, we also know that he had apparently separated out some of them for his possible probative use, prior to his recovery of the main cache. This was evidenced by the incendiary incident in the harbor in Geneva, just before Stern's return to Chamonix. So it is possible that there is a small quantity of the VS still on Earth, although none has been turned up so far in very thorough searches of Stern's *estancia* by Argentine authorities, aided by personnel from our station in the embassy in Buenos Aires. If this is true, however, and whatever may be left of this potent weapon falls into the hands of a hostile country like Russia, which is seeking to corner the world oil market, and/or those of radical terrorists wishing to settle old scores with oil-producing countries, it could set off a final doomsday scenario from which we and the rest of the world would never recover. It could pose the gravest of threats to our nation's very survival. We must never let this happen.

III. Recommendation

Accordingly, I strongly urge that we immediately deploy all available assets to ascertain whether Stern is still alive; free to act; and in

possession of any remaining VS. We must do so before any of our adversaries do or we will face one of the greatest threats ever to our nation. With your agreement, I will draw up a detailed action plan for your submission to our government's Principals for both their approval and for their operational orders to us going forward.
(s) Chris Wytham,
Director, C-TU"

****

Endlessly replaying his perception of the key events in his mind, Wytham was reasonably satisfied that, to the best of his ability, he had done what he had been charged to do. He wanted to believe that the arch villain, Albert Stern, was no more. Hadn't he seen him begin to fall to his assumed death off the vertical rock wall with his own eyes? And yet discreet inquiries with Argentine authorities had failed to establish that Stern's body had ever been found where it would have been expected to be. This was very unsettling to Wytham. He knew that glaciers were typically riven with wide fissures and crevasses, especially in the springtime. And the huge snowfall that had occurred the evening before Stern's fall might well have buried his body deep in the bowels of the Torre Glacier beneath 2 meters of fresh snow. Yet something still sat uncomfortably in Wytham's subconscious, niggling away at his sense of closure on the matter.

A report from Dick Brooks, CIO at the embassy in Buenos Aires, confirmed that both the Argentine Federal Police and the local police in El Chalten, Patagonia, had each searched Stern's *Estancia Huemul* immediately after the report of his assumed death on Cerro Torre. They had been told to look specifically for any vials of red sands that Stern might have still possessed. But they had turned up nothing.

"Chris," his deep reflection was suddenly interrupted by his secretary, "the Director is on line one."

"Good morning, Tim, what can I do for you?" Wytham asked.

"I need to meet with you and several of our senior analysts as soon as possible. We need to discuss the latest Russian energy maneuvers. Be in my office at 10:30 AM sharp, please." Director Baker replied.

"Certainly, sir." Wytham put down the phone and hastily gathered up some briefing papers from his desk.

A quick perusal of them reminded him that the cunning and despotic Russian President had won a questionable victory in the last round of national elections so as to indefinitely extend his dictatorial term as the authoritarian ruler of Russia. In the process, he had managed ruthlessly to suppress an ever more vocal but disparate opposition. Now, it seemed, he was intent both on consolidating his power centrally and restoring Russia to its former regional hegemony as the greatest of Eurasian powers. He appeared ready mercilessly to crush the plutocratic Russian Oligarchs and all others who could stand in his way, be they persons or nation States. While he knew that he could easily destabilize the former Soviet States of the "near abroad" with saber rattling and covert coercion - as he had done in the Crimea and as he was now poised to do in the Donbas Region of eastern Ukraine - his real weapon of choice for broader domination would be oil.

With Iran offline in the aftermath of its catastrophic nuclear exchange with Israel, the price of crude had remained at stratospheric levels. And the value of Russia's estimated 100 billion barrels of proved oil reserves had soared exponentially, filling the coffers of the Kremlin with an abundance of windfall wealth. At a production rate touching 11 million bbls/day, Russia was rivaling both the US and OPEC for the lead in total world production of crude oil. All of that money and oil would be potent weapons in the President's ruthless hands.

The world was still reeling from the effects of the Middle East Armageddon between Israel and Iran. Many western economies teetered on the brink of insolvency under the heavy burden of the cost of oil imports necessary for their very survival. The Euro had crashed along with the Pound Sterling. And there was little confidence left in the Dollar. World liquidity had seized up once again, more profoundly than it had in the financial crisis of 2008. Nations that could produce or import crude oil to fuel their limping economies were just barely surviving. Those that could not were facing bleak and indefinite desolation.

To add to the world's growing woes, the cloud of nuclear fallout from the Middle East had now entirely circled the globe causing endemic radiation sickness and deaths in its wake. It hung heavily above the cloud tops like an all-engrossing shroud. Temperatures plummeted worldwide, but especially in the northern hemisphere, beginning what could be a prolonged nuclear winter. The autumn harvest had failed abysmally and the early snow and ice would likely linger on the ground long into the next summer. People huddled together for warmth and sustenance. Some countries were already experiencing civil unrest stemming from the lack of adequate food, warmth and shelter. Once again, oil was at the heart of the world's woes. But Russia still had oil in abundance and it appeared ready to use it as a potent political and economic weapon. The after effects of Stern's misdeeds were still being felt worldwide. The 21st century portended bleak prospects, given the cataclysmic way it had begun.

Still in a dark, pensive mood, Wytham headed first to the cafeteria to buy a double espresso to take to the 10:30 meeting with the Director. Standing in line he noticed a slim, attractive young woman several places ahead of him. He recognized her as Talia Dagani, the very pretty Israeli Middle-Eastern analyst who had been personally sent on loan to the Agency as a goodwill gesture from Israel's national intelligence agency, the Mossad, by its new head, Chaim Levi. As she left the register with her coffee, their eyes met for a lingering moment. Then she shot Wytham a deliciously coy smile and she was off. That certainly lightened up his mood!

III

Saturday, October 27th, The Terem Palace in the Inner Kremlin, Moscow, Russia, 09:00 GMT +3

In a secluded enclave within the Kremlin complex's gem of Russian architectural and artistic culture, the Terem Palace, the President of the Russian Federation had called an extraordinary, top-secret meeting of his Inner Politburo. The walls of the ornate 19th century room were adorned with carved and painted fanciful ornaments, but its centerpiece was the most imposing: a double-headed eagle glaring imperiously down from above the head of the long, polished mahogany conference table. Once this voracious eagle was the symbol of imperial Tsarist Russia. Now it had been resurrected as the State emblem of the modern day Russian Federation.

The recent history of the re-born Russian Federation had been both quixotic and uneven. At the outset, its economy grew rapidly. In the first decade of the 2000s, soaring oil prices stimulated further exponential growth, but also encouraged increased imports, seriously overheating the economy. Everything was thus ripe for the inevitable crash triggered by the financial crisis of 2008. The Russian economy fell into a deep trough and continued to sink lower as the international price of oil fell to less than half of its previous level. Serious measures of austerity were initiated when, suddenly, unexpected salvation arrived, aided by the miscreant actions of

Albert Stern with the Viking sands. Oil prices soared once again and Russia now had the economic weapon it needed to restore it to its previous position as a world financial and geopolitical power. This fact was not lost on the President.

The President, now 69 years old, had been born into a poor Soviet family in a tough neighborhood, rife with hardship. He had to learn quickly to become a wily street fighter and scrappy underdog. But from the very outset he was quite ambitious. In the ensuing 16 years he spent as a KGB Intelligence Officer he rose quickly in influence and favor with the Communist party's *nomenklatura* before he launched himself into the meteoric rise of his political career. Muscular, but of average height, he never towered over other world leaders. Rather, he compensated for it by projecting an aura of dictatorial control and toughness, radiating through his steely-blue, reptilian eyes. A committed and ruthless authoritarian, he was also a diligent student of Russian history. His greatest regret was the shambolic dissolution years before of the former Soviet Union. Thus he had vowed to change this situation so as to restore Russian hegemony over its former vassal States.

"*Dobroye utro, kollegi.*" the President began the meeting. "Today we will begin to implement our plan for world economic domination. We shall succeed economically where the Soviet Union failed politically. We now have the oil trump card and all we need to do is skillfully and covertly to remove any of our competitors. So that, exactly, will be our course of action."

All of the President's closest confidantes present at the meeting nodded their heads in agreement, including General Ivan Chestnoy, head of the FSB security service, the successor to the KGB; General Konstantin Volkov, Chief of the General Staff of the Armed Forces; and Lieutenant General Vasili Sokolov, Commander-in-Chief of the Russian Air Force.

"Vladimir Sergeyevich," the President demanded, "do you have the current world oil production figures?"

"*Da, Gospodin President. Vot.*" Oil Minister Belyakov replied. "Total production worldwide is 80 million bbls/day. All OPEC sources dropped to 27 million bbls/day, because Iran's 4 million bbls/day are offline indefinitely after their nuclear conflict with Israel. The key swing producer, Saudi Arabia, pumped 10 million bbls/day. But the US is now at 11 million, due to their shale oil revolution. The OECD countries together produced 20 million bbls/day. The rest came from various other small producers."

"And our Russian production, Vladimir Sergeyevich?"

"We are peaking now at 10.5-11million bbls/day, *Gospodin President*."

"So if we wished to corner the world's crude oil markets we would first need selectively to remove OPEC and OECD production from the world's supply. Then we can begin to sell our oil for whatever price we wish."

"Brilliant plan, *Gospodin President.*" FSB Chief Chestnoy observed. "But how can we do this?"

"By ultimately sabotaging our biggest rivals, the Saudis and the Americans. But first we would need to take Venezuela, Angola and Nigeria offline. That would eliminate 7.5 million bbls/day. These three are soft and easy targets. We will offer their resistance organizations our covert military support and resources while we watch them destroy their countries' economies. Iran is already ruined and Iraq and Libya have never even started to recover from the chaos of their civil wars. If only we had the fearsome weapon, the Viking sands, that the Jew, Stern, unleashed on Iran, we could do it all immediately!"

"Maybe that is still possible." Chestnoy interjected. "Our covert agents embedded inside the Argentine Security Services tell us that

Stern's body has still not been recovered to this day. The glacier has been searched repeatedly. Perhaps he survived? Maybe he still has some of the weapon left?"

"That would be ideal, *Vanya!*" the President replied, slipping into the diminutive form of address. "We must try to find Stern if he is still alive. I would think that he must have kept some of the Viking sands in reserve as an insurance policy for his future safety. A small amount is all that we would need. We know that none of it will be forthcoming from the original Martian source in the immediate future."

"*Pravilna.*" the Defense Minister agreed, "The UN Resolution that banned all future flights to Mars will be rigorously enforced by the US. They have X37-B space vehicles with powerful laser cannons in orbit to annihilate any spacecraft trying to break free of Earth orbit."

"That's still to be tested, *tovarisch*, but it would be easier first to find Stern, if he is still with us."

"But where would we start looking?" Chestnoy wondered out loud.

"That will be for your FSB to figure out, *Vanya*. But whatever it takes, you must do it soon! First, though, we need to block the Straits of Hormuz, further to drive up oil prices in advance of our first crude auction." the President continued. "Admiral Zharkov, find an old container ship and have it loaded to capacity with empty containers. There are only to be high-intensity incendiary devices primed and located inside each container. Send it to the Persian Gulf, near to the opening of the Straits. Then track all VLCC crude carriers with full cargoes about to navigate through them. Our container ship will suddenly lose its steering mechanism and collide violently with a loaded VLCC. A full cargo of oil; an explosion; and an ensuing fire should ensure that both ships sink in the Straits, blocking transit through them indefinitely. Try to rescue any of our survivors by submarine. Those we lose, however, will have made a commendable sacrifice for the Motherland."

"*Ponimat, Gospodin President.* But what if the VLCC is US-flagged or under their protection? We could provoke a serious international incident."

"I am not worried about that, *tovarisch* Admiral. The American President is a neophyte idiot on whom we have a full dossier of salacious *kompromat*. Besides, we did more than enough to help him get elected. We can bring him down anytime we choose. In an instant we can shut down his entire country and he knows it. On my orders our cyber trolls can wreak total havoc on the Americans' nuclear, electric power and water infrastructures. We can send them back to the Stone Age! He will posture and whimper, but he won't act. And stupidly, he still thinks that we are his friends!"

With that final remark the President abruptly adjourned the meeting.

IV

Wednesday, October 24th, Estancia Huemul outside of El Chalten, Patagonia, Argentina, 11:00 GMT -4

Carlos, the old *gaucho*, was stunned when Albert walked through the front door of the *estancia*. "*Señor* Lopez?" he said, eyes wide with fright. "But you are...."

"*Muerto*, Carlos? I'm afraid that reports of my death were greatly exaggerated."

"But Cristian told me of your fall. *Alabado sea Dios*! It's a miracle! The El Chalten police along with the *Federales* were just here, early this morning, searching the *estancia*. I don't know what they were looking for though."

"I can't even guess, but never mind. I need some quiet time to think. No one must know that I am here! Where are the other *gauchos*, Carlos?"

"It's spring planting season, *Señor*. They have all returned to their *granjas pobres* to put in their new crops. I'm the only one here for now."

That was exactly what Albert wanted to hear. The fewer the people who knew of his survival, the better, although he wasn't at all sure of why. In any event, Carlos was already one too many. Albert intuitively knew that he would have to deal with that soon.

Albert was quite disturbed by the fact that both the local police and the Argentine *Federales* had come to search his *estancia*. He couldn't imagine what they were looking for. Entering his master bedroom suite he could see immediately that it had been thoroughly tossed and combed through. Everything was in complete disarray. What he couldn't have known though was that the CIA had been in touch with the Argentine Security Service about the remote possibility of there being even the minutest remnants of the Viking sands somewhere in Albert's personal effects. If so, they would be the only ones left on Earth. The sight of the mess instinctively stirred Albert into action.

Being sure that Carlos was out of visual range, Albert found himself impulsively drawn to open up his old rucksack that he had used while hiking in Chamonix. He rummaged through its contents. He seemed to be searching for something very specific, although he couldn't remember what it was. Finally his hand found his travel kit where he had earlier hidden a small quantity of the Viking sands as an insurance policy for his own self-preservation. From inside the cylindrical tube of an almost empty, push-up Polo deodorant stick two small vials of red sand fell out. Interpol hadn't found them on the train ride back from Chamonix nor had the Argentine authorities earlier that day. Some of it had been used up to destroy the yacht, *Jolie Mademoiselle*, in the Geneva harbor, but there was still an ample 50 grams left, divided between the two vials.

Albert looked pensively at the vials of deep red granules that could either prove to be his salvation or his ultimate doom. He struggled hard to put them into context. Yet only dim flickers of recognition and remembrance seemed to flit through his consciousness, like still frames plucked from a grainy old black and white movie. What was the significance of these seemingly harmless vials of red sand, he wondered? Why did he have them hidden away? Why were the authorities so anxious to search his home? What were they looking for? Surely not just for vials of sand! What was becoming clear to him, though, was that for reasons unknown, he was a hunted man. Sadly, he thought, it meant that he'd probably have to leave Argentine Patagonia quite soon. But before he did his instincts told him that he had to secure the enigmatic sands in such a way as to leave a portion behind, well hidden. If he ever needed them again - for whatever purpose he could not then imagine - they would be there.

"Carlos," Albert said as he returned to the *estancia's* great room, "call *Expediciones Exupery* in El Chalten and ask for my guide, Cristian Rodrigues. Tell him that you must speak urgently with him in person out here, at the *estancia*. But don't tell him that I am here too, *mi entiendes?*"

"*Si, Señor, claro*. I will do it immediately."

V

Friday, October 26th, Director of Intelligence Baker's Office, CIA Headquarters, Langley, Virginia, 10:30 EDT

As Wytham entered Director Baker's office the chief was already

THE VIKING SANDS : ENDGAME

in discussion with several analysts from the Russian Desk of the Euro Division. This tall, slim and courtly Princetonian in his early 60s had been an Establishment fixture in DC for many years. Long, dark hair parted neatly down the middle and a pair of old fashioned tortoise shell glasses framed his wizened face. Many thought of him as a later day clone of Robert McNamara.

"Come in and have a seat, Chris, we were just starting our analysis." Baker invited.

One of the more senior analysts started by describing what the Russians had recently done to ratchet up the level of energy deprivation in western Europe. "They have all but shut down oil and natural gas exports through their *Druzhba*, Brotherhood, *Soyuz*, Jamal, South Stream and Nord Stream 1 pipelines direct to Western Europe and Turkey. They say it's routine maintenance, but they have never before had so many pipelines offline at one time."

"Yes, and I understand that they've announced that they won't honor benchmark posted oil prices in Platts Crude Oil Marketwire anymore. Instead they intend to sell limited quantities of crude oil to the highest daily bidders in a Dutch auction, effective immediately."

"But that will finally tip the world over into a deep depression." Wytham exclaimed. "Crude is already very scarce and selling, when available, for over $500/bbl."

"I know, Chris, but we are trying to counter the Russians' bear hug by asking our Saudi allies further to ramp up their production." Baker interjected. "They still have several million barrels daily of spare capacity. Without them, we're all sunk."

"But will they do it, Tim? And are their facilities secure against sabotage? Anything can happen in today's chaotic world."

"That's what we are trying to find out, Chris. For what it is worth, the President talked personally by phone with both the Saudi King and his Oil Minister just yesterday. We're putting on a

17

full-court press. But I worry too about security for their reserves and delivery systems. There are a lot of bad actors out there that see this as a chance to topple the octogenarian Saudi monarchy once and for all. We've offered them our covert assistance, but we'll just have to wait and see."

"How do our assets embedded inside the FSB read the latest Russian maneuvers, Tim?"

"That's a very sensitive issue right now, Chris. Several of them have recently been outed. Colonel Valery Voronov was just convicted of spying for us and he was sentenced to 20 years hard labor in a Siberian *gulag*. There had been a few others caught before him. Our relations with the Russians are more tense than ever."

"But of course we exercised plausible deniability over the Voronov incident, right, Tim?"

"Yes, Chris, but for now, our covert assets are running for cover. We're not getting the reliable feedback we desperately need. Anyway, that's how things stand today. I suggest that we reconvene later this week if we get some fresh intel from our Russian operatives. By the way, Chris," Baker continued, "I did a quick read of your Trip Report and I am considering your recommendations. Do you really think that there is any chance that Stern is still alive and in possession of any more of the Viking sands? It certainly seems like a very long shot."

"Be that as it may, Tim, it's not a risk we can afford to take. I believe that we should move forward quickly to find out, as I have suggested." A number of the analysts present nodded in agreement.

"I will certainly take it under advisement, Chris." Baker replied.

As the meeting broke up Director Baker asked Wytham to stay on for a moment. "Chris," Baker asked, "have you met Talia Dagani yet, our Israeli Middle East analyst on loan to us from the Mossad?"

"No, Tim, not formally."

"Well go introduce yourself and get with her. She has some very valuable intel on the security systems the Saudis use to safeguard their oilfields and pipelines. You would expect that the Israelis have been studying that very carefully for a long time."

"Certainly, Tim. I'll do it right away."

The morning seemed to be getting better for Wytham every minute!

VI

Thursday, October 25th, 2012, Estancia Huemul outside of El Chalten, Patagonia, Argentina, 09:00 GMT -4

"*Buenas días*, Cristian." Carlos greeted the wiry guide as he walked in the front door of the *estancia*. "Someone here wants to talk privately with you."

As Albert walked out of his bedroom, Cristian's face went ashen white.

"*Dios mio, un fantasma!*" he gasped.

"No, Cristian, I'm not a ghost. I am very much alive." Albert reassured the frightened young man. "I know that it's hard to believe, but, miraculously, I survived the fall."

"I am so very sorry about what happened, *Señor* Lopez, I couldn't hold you. I am sure you realize that." Cristian stammered in fright.

"I don't blame you, Cristian, it was just a climbing accident. Sit down and have a coffee and some *medialunas*. I will need your guiding services again soon." Relieved, Cristian sat down to listen.

"I absolutely must go to Chile for a while, unobserved." Albert began. "Not by plane, bus or car. The only way is on foot from here."

"But that would mean crossing the *Campo de Hielo Sur* - the Great Southern Ice Cap - *Señor*. It's a very long, hard and dangerous trek. It's 65 kilometers from east to west."

"Yes, I know, but you have some experience with the route, right?"

"I have taken clients before as far as *Circos de los Altares* and to climb the volcano, Cerro Lautoro, but never all the way across to Chile."

"Well, Cristian, this time we will have to make it all the way there. But this must be kept *very* secret. You must not tell *Expediciones Exupery* that you are going to Chile or with whom. That is imperative, *tu entiendes*? You will just tell them that you have a new client who wants a full experience of the Great Southern Ice Cap. Whatever your daily rate is, I will triple it. When we arrive in Chile I will get you an air ticket back to El Calafate and pay you for your taxi ride home to El Chalten, agreed?" But Cristian could never have imagined that he might only be making a one-way trip.

"*Convenido, Señor.* When shall we set out?"

"In about a week's time, Cristian. I have a few things that need attending to here first. Here's an advance in *pesos*. Start buying us the necessary provisions and equipment and be ready to go when I call you."

VII

Albert had one more important thing to do before he set out with Cristian across the Great Southern Ice Cap. He had to be sure that no one in El Chalten knew that he was still alive. In this regard, the old *gaucho* caretaker, Carlos, was still an inconvenient problem.

When it came to the thought of killing Carlos, Albert seemed to be guided by instinct. It was as if a dark side of him that he couldn't remember was acting on autopilot. Had he killed before? He didn't know. But he felt no compunction at all about dispatching the old *gaucho* if it was a question of his own survival. At least one part of Albert Stern's sociopathic personality was completely intact. He could still kill without emotion or remorse. He would feel nothing; just a familiar empty void.

"Carlos", Albert called, "have you fixed the electrical short yet in the sheep-shearing shed? It's still causing lights to flicker here in the main house."

"Not yet, *Señor*, but I was just heading over there to work on it. Can you shut the main breaker off, please, while I attend to it?"

"OK, but be careful!"

Albert watched Carlos enter the shed from a facing window. It was dark and damp inside with patches of standing water on the floor. Carlos took a flashlight with him along with some tools and electrical tape to attend to the frayed wiring. Soon he was standing in a puddle with shears in his hand to cut and patch the frayed circuit. Just as Carlos' two hands engaged the wire, Albert remorselessly flipped back on the main breaker. As the old man shuddered violently and fell to the floor dead, Albert knew that his unexpected return to life in El Chalten was a limited secret once again. It would be weeks before the other *gauchos* returned to the *estancia* from their spring plantings to find Carlos' body. There was still Cristian who knew of Albert's seeming resurrection, but Albert knew that he would have to deal with him as well, soon enough.

VIII

Thursday, November 1st, Paso Marconi west of El Chalten, Patagonia, Argentina, 07:00 GMT -4

After a long, steep ascent through the *lenga* forests of the Rio Electrico valley, skirting Lago Electrico, Cristian and Albert finally arrived at the foot of the Marconi Glacier, at the eastern snout of the Great Southern Ice Cap. Another hard slog up a precipitous field of slippery scree on the glacier's moraine led them onto the *Campo de Hielo Sur* itself. Once they were on the ice they donned their crampons and then roped-up to protect each other from falling into hidden crevasses. The day was clear and the wind was unusually gentle for a Patagonian spring. Thirty five kilometers away to the northwest they could see the top of the active volcano, Cerro Lautoro, peaking out of the vast expanse of snow. Sulfur fumes belched from its top and mixed with the clouds streaming from its summit ridges. But the vastness of the white expanse before them made it look deceptively close, like a shimmering mirage. To the south and quite nearby were the rarely seen west faces of both Mt. Fitzroy and Cerro Torro. Seeing the latter gave Albert a real shiver. Behind Cerro Lautoro and the nameless mountains on the horizon, there was no human habitation until the ice cap met the Pacific Ocean, 30 kilometers further on in Chile.

Under the best possible weather conditions the trek would take at least a week, averaging optimally about 10 kilometers a day. That would be, of course, if both snow and fog, as well as the strong winds generated far out in the Pacific that often race across the ice cap at incredible speeds, didn't impede them. The latter, known as the *Escoba de Dios* – "God's Broom" – could exceed 200 kilometers/hour, putting anyone or anything on the ice cap at their complete mercy.

But so far the weather was fine and the long journey to yet another unknown twist of fate was underway for Albert. What would he encounter in Chile, assuming that he made it safely there? Who was investigating and pursuing him and why? Why couldn't he remember anything of his past life? What of the small vial of red sand granules that he had instinctively packed so carefully to take along with him, while caching the other in an unlikely but secure place at the *estancia*? Why was it so important? When would it all come clear again to him? These were the thoughts that raced continuously through Albert's head as he listened to the crunch of his crampons biting into the thickly crusted snow with each of his labored steps. But most immediately, he thought, how and when would he deal with the problem of silencing Cristian forever before the long, hard journey was done?

PART 2
THE DOUBLE-HEADED EAGLE

"Even in the ashes there are a few sparks."

I

Sunday, November 11th, El Chalten, Patagonia, Argentina, 23:00 GMT -4

Colonel Viktor Borisenko and Major Arkady Fortunatov, both of the FSB, arrived late in El Chalten after a jarring taxi ride across die-straight, gravel-topped roads leading from El Calafate. They were both tired and choking incessantly on the dust that had been thrown up as wake by the old taxi's tires. They had been sent personally to this little hamlet nestled hard up against the eastern edge of the Great Southern Ice Cap by FSB head, General Ivan Chestnoy. Their covert mission was to find Albert Stern, if he was still alive. Both men were former KGB veterans specializing in "wet work" – torture, rendition and political assassination.

"Just like where the steppe meets the southern Urals, eh, *Arkasha*?" Borisenko observed through weary eyes.

"*Da*, Colonel. Let's check-in and get some sleep."

The two men checked into the Hosteria el Puma on the outskirts of the small but haphazardly growing town. The next day they would start their discrete inquiries with the local provincial police. The plan was to pose as insurance company inspectors who needed to verify the death of one of their insureds. Tall and fit, Fortunatov was fluent in both Spanish and English. Stubby and muscular, Borisenko had a good passing knowledge of both languages as well. They would maintain that a two million dollar life insurance policy had been taken out by "Alberto Portillo Lopez", but no valid death certificate had ever been submitted by his heirs. The hope was that someone in El Chalten knew of Lopez's (Stern's) survival and whereabouts. It was a long shot for sure.

II

"*Buenos dias.*" Fortunatov greeted the Chief Inspector for Santa Cruz Province at his office early the next morning.
"*Bienvenidos, Señor.* How can I help you?"
"We are claims agents from Santander Seguros life insurance company in Madrid. We are investigating the alleged death of one of our insureds. His heirs are claiming the full benefit of a very large life policy, *Señor*, but we have not yet seen a valid death certificate. Allegedly, he died on Tuesday, October 23rd, in a fall from a sheer rock wall on Cerro Torre. His name is Alberto Portillo Lopez. Do you have a police report that we can see, please, on this incident?"
"Ah yes, the Lopez climbing incident. Here is the report. As you can see, the whole matter is quite an enigma. *Señor* Lopez's local guide, Cristian Rodrigues, reported his fall and presumed death, but we have never found the victim's body to corroborate the story. We have searched the glacier repeatedly beneath the rock face to no avail. We can only assume that the body fell into a deep crevasse and that it will not be seen again for many years. They do all eventually reappear at the glacier's terminal moraine, sometimes 50 years later."
"So no final death certificate was ever issued by the coroner's office, correct?"
"*Si, Señor.* It was not possible to do so."
"And this local guide – Cristian Rodrigues – where can we find

him, please?"

"He works for *Expediciones Exupery* here in town, but he has unfortunately disappeared for almost a fortnight now. He was last heard of to be taking a very confidential client for an extended trek on the *Campo de Hielo Sur*. You can talk with their manager if you'd like, *Señor*. Their offices are only just a few streets away from here."

The two men thanked the inspector and headed over to *Expediciones Exupery*. After introducing themselves they enquired about any news of Cristian Rodrigues. Where had he gone and with whom? When was he last seen? Did he have a satellite phone and when did he last check-in?

"All very puzzling." the manager said. "Not at all like him. He is one of our most careful guides. He is always very diligent about keeping us informed. But this time he was particularly reticent about his client's identity and their ultimate destination. I believe they were going to cross over the Ice Cap, well into Chile. He was here just before he departed, buying supplies. He took one of our sledges for ice crossings, as well as a satellite phone. Earlier he had been out at the *Estancia Huemul*, but it must have been to visit an old *gaucho* friend. You heard, no doubt, that the *patron*, *Señor* Lopez, Cristian's former client, is assumed to have tragically died when he fell from the east face of Cerro Torre."

"Did Rodrigues leave any information about his current client?" Fortunatov pressed. "Any details at all?"

"No, *Señor*. Normally we require all of our guides to complete a full, intended itinerary sheet with the names and copies of the identity cards or passports of all of their clients, but Cristian was quite adamant that he wouldn't do so. It was all very secretive and enigmatic. He just told us to trust him; he'd be back in a few weeks time. That was the last we saw of or heard from him. *Que mala suerte*! He is one of our very best guides."

III

Back at the Hosteleria del Puma, Borisenko locked the door to the suite that he and Fortunatov occupied. Then he took out his iPad. It had been specially encrypted and re-engineered to provide a secure, direct link to his superiors at the FSB in Moscow. Connected by satellite, he punched in his coded username, *Medved*, and password. After being granted top-secret access, he began to type an urgent message to FSB chief Chestnoy:

"Local police cannot confirm Stern's death. No remains were ever found. His guide during the climbing accident is now on a two-week trek across the Great Southern Ice Cap, heading to Chile with a single client. Secretive nature of this journey opens the possibility that the guide's client is Stern, escaping inquiries in Argentina by their Secret Security Service. Likely route is across Marconi Glacier onto Great Southern Ice Cap; NW towards Cerro Lautoro volcano; crossing into Chile in Bernardo O'Higgins National Park; and then due W towards the fjords around Wellington Island in Chile. Nearest Chilean city of any size is Puerto Natales to the south. From there subject(s) can board a coastal cruiser to anywhere along the Chilean coast. *Urgently* request immediate deployment of surveillance capabilities of the nearest Kobalt-M optical reconnaissance satellite to pinpoint location of subjects on the Ice Cap. Their ultimate disposition to be ordered by you after their location coordinates are confirmed. (s) "*M*"

The Kobalt-M reconnaissance optical reconnaissance satellite was one of a series of high-resolution, low Earth orbit spy satellites capable of modifying its orbital path multiple times in order to capture images of its chosen targets. Nominal resolution is 2 meters, but by making descent maneuvers using its propulsion unit, the satellite can produce images with a resolution that reaches 0.3

meters. The satellite's images are used by the Russian Ministry of Defense, the Main Intelligence Directorate of the Chief of Staff and the FSB. The superior optical capabilities of the Kobalt-M made it the surveillance instrument perfectly suited to locate and identify a party of two persons attempting to cross the vast *Campo de Hielo Sur*.

Within minutes Chestnoy, codenamed *Natchalnik*, replied to Borisenko from Moscow:

"Kobalt-M surveillance to be mobilized immediately. Urgently assessing feasibility of intrusion into Argentine or Chilean air space with stealth aircraft for sanction. You are ordered to proceed immediately to Puerto Natales to await further orders once subjects have been located and tracked. Stern will be taken alive, if possible, for rendition to Moscow. His guide will be eliminated. More when location and identity are confirmed. (s) *"N"*

Borisenko read the message and shot a satisfied grin at the curious Fortunatov. "We shall be on the move again soon, *Arkasha*."

IV

Monday, November 12th, On The Great Southern Icecap, Patagonia, Between Argentina and Chile, 15:00 GMT -4

Ten kilometers a day had been far too ambitious a goal for crossing the Great Southern Ice Cap. The pair were already 5 days behind schedule. Just west of Cerro Lautoro, Albert and Cristian had been completely stalled and tent-bound for 2 days in a howling whiteout. The fearsome *Escobado de Dias* was sweeping the frigid glacier's surface clean, generating suffocating spindrift devils that penetrated their tent and filled their eyes and nostrils with choking micro particles of ice.

"At least another four days, *Señor*, if the storm lets up." Cristian ventured. "We will make no progress today and our supplies are beginning to run low." With that he crawled out of the tent to re-secure the ice pitons holding down their heavy duty Mountain Hardware tent against the howling tempest.

"*Señor* Lopez", Cristian suddenly cried out above the gale, "I see something very unusual approaching us from the west. It is flying low across the *Campo*. It is heading right for us!"

Albert looked out of the tent flap and saw the apparition approaching as well. What could it possibly be? Nothing ever flew over the Great Southern Ice Cap except the rare Argentine or Chilean military aircraft on training runs. It was otherwise absolutely forbidden by both countries. He was completely puzzled.

As the unexpected visitor got closer its configuration identified it as a black helicopter. Not just any helicopter though. Neither Albert nor Cristian would know it but it was a Russian-made 5th generation Kamov Ka-58 Black Ghost stealth military chopper. It was state-of-the-art at evading radar and it bristled with lethal armaments. After years of development it had been refined into a stealth platform that had a radar profile no larger than that of a small starling. It was virtually undetectable. Launched from a Russian navy cruiser masquerading as an oceanic research boat in the Pacific Ocean off Chile, it had flown very low under Chilean radar as a final precaution. And now there it was, about to land feet away from Albert and Cristian on the snow covered glacier.

Shielding his freezing hands and face from the prop wash, Albert saw two white clad figures emerge from the muffled, idling chopper. Both carried AK-47 Kalashnikov assault rifles at the ready.

"Come with us immediately, Stern." one of them said gruffly, in heavily Eastern European-accented English. To Albert's complete amazement and shock, the other fired a lethal burst at Cristian, killing him instantly. The intruders had suddenly and surgically done what Albert knew he had to do later anyway, but that was, to say the least, of no comfort to him now. Albert tried to reply but he was completely frozen with fear. Finally he managed to stammer "Stern? Who is Stern? You are making a terrible mistake! I am Alberto Portillo Lopez and...."

"Shut up, собака!" barked the operative in command. "We both know who you are." With that he approached the terrified Albert and shoved the nozzle of his Kalashnikov against the base of his skull. Roughly his colleague grabbed Albert's arms and secured them tightly behind his back with plastic handcuff strips. "марш!, march!" he barked. Albert had intuitively understood the first time and helplessly complied.

As Albert was being led toward the waiting chopper the other operative dragged Cristian's body over to a nearby, yawning crevasse and dumped it in. Then he covered the area where Cristian had fallen with fresh snow to hide the bloodstains. Anyone coming to look for the camp would find it undisturbed but completely empty.

The last thing Albert remembered as he puzzled over the sudden dire turn of events was a stifling hood being secured over his head and the sharp pinprick of a needle through his hiking pants into his right buttock. After that all went quickly black.

V

Wednesday, November 14th, CIA Headquarters, Langley, Virginia, 09:00 EST

Chris Wytham looked up from his desk to see the lovely silhouette of Talia Dagani framed in his office doorway. "What a delightful surprise!" he thought. He had finally met her over coffee and he was completely smitten by her incredible looks and charm. Lustrous, long dark hair; big, expressive brown eyes; slim hips; toned, shapely legs; and large, generous breasts, all packaged neatly into a 5'2", 116 lb. frame. Everything for which a man could wish!

But unlike her earlier, coyly flirtatious demeanor, Dagani was all business today. "Chris, I have had some disturbing intel that just came in from Mossad HQ in Herzliya. It came directly from Director Chaim Levi's office. Our operatives infiltrated into the Russian FSB reported that Stern is both alive and securely in FSB hands on a disguised Russian navy warship, just off the coast of Chile. Can you believe that?"

"Never! No way! I saw him fall off the cliff with my own eyes. He surely must have died!"

"You saw him fall, Chris, but did you see him land fatally on the glacier below? You know that to this day his body has never been found."

"I saw him fall part of the way before a shroud of clouds enveloped the view. The wind was blowing furiously up the face. But he could never have survived such a fall. I'm guessing that the howling tempest must have driven him forcefully against the hard granite wall several times on his way down. No one could have lived through that!"

"But, evidently, he did. We have unimpeachable evidence that the Russians have him and, possibly, any remaining Viking sands that he might have still had with him. You can be sure that he will be rendered to Moscow as quickly as possible."

"That's quite incredible, Talia. But he couldn't have any of the sands left at all. They were all scattered to the wind in Chamonix and the only other remaining source went down in flames in the hold of Viking 4 when it crashed into the Iranian oil complex on Kharg Island."

"Don't be so sure, Chris. Remember that when he stashed them in Chamonix he had clearly kept a small quantity in reserve to prove their potency to us. He had at least enough separately to do in the pleasure yacht in the harbor in Geneva. He's a wily, paranoid creature who is always careful to protect his own back. So if he still had some of the sands, despite the Argentine Security Service's thorough search of his *estancia* in El Chalten, they're now probably in Russian hands. Given the ruthless squeeze the Russians are now putting on the world's market for crude oil, such a weapon at their disposal could annihilate all of the reserves of their oil-producing rivals, including those of your country, in short order. It all adds up to the worst possible scenario!"

"Christ, Talia, that's devastating, if true. We need to discuss this urgently with Director Baker. Gather up our analysts while I call over to Baker's office to request an immediate appointment. We may not have any time to lose!"

VI

Thursday, November 15th, Aboard Russian Oceanic Research Ship "Glasnost", off the coast of Chilean Patagonia, 10:00 GMT -4

Albert awoke to the blinding glare of a high-powered light shining directly into his weary eyes. The sedative that he had been given was only just wearing off, revealing to him his uncomfortable plight. Tightly bound and strapped into a hard wooden chair, he was vaguely aware of the gentle roll of the ship as it sat at anchor just outside of Chilean territorial waters.

Without warning, a vicious slap from an unseen assailant snapped him into full consciousness and focused his attention. "So, Stern, where is the weapon?" a heavily accented Slavic voice asked. Shocked and confused, Albert stammered back "Stern? Weapon? I don't know what you mean! I am Alberto Portillo Lopez, an Argentine *estanciero*, and I know nothing of any weapon."

"Liar!" the interrogator snarled. He was a seasoned, KGB-trained operative who knew that he mustn't fail in this mission. If Stern wouldn't talk now he and his associate knew many intricate, torturous ways with which to coax the truth out of him. Stern would be begging to cooperate once they were finished with him.

"Major," said another voice from the shadows, "we have searched him and his belongings thoroughly and we haven't found anything. He must have stashed it somewhere for safekeeping. Shall I beat it out of him now or should we just shoot him and get it over with?"

"*Nyet*, Dimitri, you *debyl*, our orders were to get the weapon if he has it and then to arrange rendition of them both to Moscow. But if he hasn't got the weapon, we can dispose of him however we would like. A shot in the head and a weighted bag into the sea, perhaps?" The Major had pointedly said this to be sure that Albert heard it, loud and clear.

Sensing his imminent demise, Albert decided to cooperate, although he wasn't sure exactly how. "Tell me, please, what you are looking for amongst my meager possessions. I can find it for you."

"The weapon. The sands. You have some left, no? Where are they, you filthy *sobaka*?"

Suddenly it was clear to Albert. The enigmatic sands; is that what they wanted? He vaguely sensed that they were significant, but he still had no idea why. Let them have them, then! He had no use for them.

"In my rucksack, amongst my toiletries. A push-up deodorant stick. Inside there is a vial. You will see."

"Only one vial? Have another look, Dimitri. If he is right we must let Moscow know immediately. Then we can all go home. But first take several digital pictures of his face to send off to the FSB's central database at the Integrated Center for Data Processing and Storage in Moscow. You know, just follow standard procedures." the Major concluded disinterestedly.

Deep down in his subconscious Stern knew that he had wisely cached the last existing vial of Viking sands in a secure and unlikely place at the *estancia*. He had felt he might need the enigmatic sands again, but he had no idea why. Calamitously, though, under extreme fear of imminent death, he had been coerced finally to admit their additional existence to his captors. While they knew they could not then access this last cache, they had dutifully informed Moscow of its existence.

VII

Wednesday, November 14th , CIA Headquarters, Langley, Virginia, 10:00 EST

A deep furrow of concern creased Director Baker's brow as he called the hastily scheduled meeting to order. "Chris, if the intel Talia received from the Mossad is true, it defies all logic!"

"Surely you know that our intel is always accurate and fully-vetted, Director." Dagani interjected, somewhat testily.

"Stay calm, Talia. I have a lot of respect for the thoroughness with which the Mossad operates. But we have our own protocols to follow. We will need independent verification from our own sources. Ideally from at least two."

"Things are on a razor's edge with Moscow, Tim," said Wytham, "but we are already trying to contact our covert operatives inside the FSB. We should get confirmation or, at least, the Russians' plausible denial from them soon."

"Something is afoot with the Russians in Chile." the Director continued. "After the 7.2 earthquake there in the south last week the Russians sent them an AN-225 cargo plane full of humanitarian supplies and rescue equipment. They are certainly not known for such magnanimous gestures. There must be something – or somebody – there that they want."

All of a sudden the door of the Director's office burst unexpectedly open to reveal the figure of an agitated young analyst. "Sorry, sir! Please excuse my intrusion, but there is some new, raw footage from a NAVSTAR 2-F satellite taken recently over Patagonia that you need to see urgently."

"It better be relevant to our discussions." Baker said with annoyance. "Put it up on the big screen and let's all have a look."

As the lights dimmed the large LED monitor first displayed a vast, featureless desert of white that was clearly the Great Southern Ice Cap between Argentina and Chile. Then a black apparition appeared at the top of the screen, coming in low from the west. Like a giant dragonfly it flew along the snow-covered glacier, heading towards what appeared to be a campsite with a single tent and two figures standing near it in startled attention. Zooming in with incredible resolution, the spy satellite's camera lenses were able to identify the craft as a Russian military Kamov Ka-58 Black Ghost stealth helicopter. As it came to a halt nearby, two white-clad, armed men jumped out. With dispatch they killed one of the two glacier trekkers and then bound and hooded the other. It all happened at high speed. In a matter of moments the chopper was gone, leaving only the vast expanse of white nothingness to fill the screen.

"We were able to zoom in on the man they took away, sir," the young analyst said, "and we believe that it was Albert Stern."

"Well, if it really was him, we can't let them keep him!" Baker declared. "We have no choice but to extract him immediately and bring him home for detailed interrogation."

VIII

Friday, November 16th, Aboard USN Virginia Class Attack Submarine "Patrick Henry", off the coast of Chilean Patagonia, 23:00 GMT -4

"Run silent, run deep." This was the mission statement of the US Navy's Virginia class SSN-774 nuclear-powered, fast-attack stealth sub, *"Patrick Henry"*. It was amply armed with the latest in intelligence-gathering capabilities and weapons systems technology. Submerged with only its slender photonic observation mast above water, it lay just abeam of the disguised Russian navy ship, *"Glasnost"*, at a distance of a quarter of a mile. Silently, it was watching it under a black, moonless sky. On board with the regular crew was a Navy Seal Team 6 squad, the service's most elite hunter-killers. They were who would carry out the planned extraction of Albert Stern.

"All quiet aboard the target, Captain." the sub's XO reported. "Ready to deploy the extraction team on your command."

"Roger that. Bring us up to the surface to launch the Zodiac boats. Is the team assembled for a go? Are the nerve gas canisters and launchers at the ready?"

"Affirmative, sir. All is in place for full deployment."

The hatch opened above the conning tower and the seals, dressed in black wetsuits, emerged. They were to be led by Commander Craig Shultze, a barrel-chested, seasoned veteran of many such covert extraction operations. He proceeded to brief the team on how events should successfully unfold.

"We will approach the target towards the stern, out of view of the bridge and away from regular security patrols. When we are within range - about 100 yards – we'll fire the nerve gas canisters in an all-enveloping pattern. You will put your gas masks on immediately and then a brief wait. The gas acts almost instantaneously and it should swiftly and completely debilitate all aboard. Once on deck we move quickly to find our man. Try not to fire at or kill anyone. It shouldn't be necessary. We need to avoid doing obvious harm so as to maintain the plausible deniability of our mission. All understood?"

"Aye, sir!" the team chorused back. "But how so?" asked E-6 petty officer Murphy.

"The Russians will never admit to the real mission of their ship nor that they had Stern aboard. The nerve gas will render the officers and crew unconscious while we do the extraction. So if we do this right we were never there. No one onboard will ever see or hear us. They will just awake later with bad headaches and with one less prisoner. There's our government's plausible deniability, got it? Ready then? Let's go!" Schultze ordered.

The electric motored zodiacs proceeded silently toward the stern of the *Glasnost*. The nerve gas canisters would be fired from compressed air guns, making no real sound. They would explode with a dull thud, blanketing the ship with the sickening, fast-acting gas. The crew would drop in place like flies. The Russians would later realize what had been used on them, as it was the same, very effective, fentanyl-based agent that they had deployed against the terrorists in the Moscow theatre siege of 2002. As a critical added benefit, the odorless, colorless gas had a temporary amnesiac effect on all those who breathed it in.

Undetected, the team launched the canisters. A few minutes later they fired grappling hooks with rope ladders attached over the ship's stern railings. Quickly they clamored aboard and began to fan out in a detailed search pattern. The few ship's sentries lay unconscious on the deck. All officers and hands on the bridge were similarly immobilized.

THE VIKING SANDS : ENDGAME

"Commander, sir, we are heading towards the brig." one squad leader reported. An all-purpose lock-picking tool easily opened the brig's bulkhead door. There, inside, sat a hooded man, head slumped to his chest. Bound hands and feet to a captain's chair, it was clearly Stern.

"Got him!" said the squad leader. "Cut him loose and we'll carry him up to the deck. Leave the hood on his head and handcuff his hands behind his back with this plastic tether." They proceeded to do so with dispatch. The whole operation had taken only 8 minutes so far.

On deck Commander Schultze coordinated the movements of his own squad. All seemed to be going well when suddenly he heard heavy, unexpected footsteps behind him. Staggering as if severely drunk, a huge, burly crewman was heading towards him armed with a standard Russian Navy military issue G-Sh-18 9X19mm Parabellum pistol. As he tried to steady himself for a headshot at Schultze, squad member Murphy swiftly leveled him from behind with a vicious karate chop to the back of his neck.

Grateful to be saved, it nevertheless posed a real dilemma for Schultze. What to do with this man? Only one in a million could withstand the full and immediate effects of the potent nerve gas, but this man was apparently one such. And if the amnesiac effect of the chemical agent failed to work on him he would be a live witness to what otherwise would have been a perfect covert operation.

"We have no option but to kill and dispose of him, Murphy." Schultze said decisively. "He's out cold. Strip him of any ID he may be carrying. Then lean him over the ship's railings, cut his throat and drop him overboard. But be careful not to let any blood fall on the deck! We will let Mother Nature help us do the rest."

It was imperative that the sailor's body never be recovered intact later on the Chilean shore. But this was a *La Niña* year in the eastern

39

Pacific, bringing colder surface waters closer to the mainland. And with it came deep-sea predators that otherwise wouldn't approach the continental landmass so closely. Amongst them were schools of predacious Humboldt squid and vicious hunting packs of bull, mako and tiger sharks with rapacious appetites for blood. They would do the final disposal job with great efficiency.

The unexpected "wet work" concluded, Stern was lowered into an awaiting Zodiac raft as the rest of the team clamored back down the rope ladders behind him. Grapples removed from the ship's rails, they motored away back towards the waiting *Patrick Henry*, leaving no visible trace of their brief presence behind. Mission accomplished so far.

IX

Albert could remember little or nothing of his rendition back to the United States. Hooded and handcuffed, he was vaguely aware of being lowered by rope down the side of the Russian vessel into a smaller boat, running silently and swiftly on an electric motor. It bounced wildly over the swells until coming abruptly to a halt besides what sounded from its mooring approach like the hull of a large metal craft. Muffled noises told him that a hatch had been opened above him and a rope ladder had been lowered down to the Zodiac boat. He was placed roughly into a hoisting sling while the remaining crew scrambled up the ladder. At the top of the sub's conning tower he felt a new set of hands on him as he was guided down steps and marched along a fairly narrow passageway to the end of a short corridor. He could hear a metal door clang open and then he was pushed into a small, unlit room. Before he could sense anything else about his new surroundings he felt a sharp prick in his shoulder as a syringe full of fast-acting sedative was administered to him. He barely was able to slump down onto the rough, hard cot to which he was guided before he was fully out cold.

X

"Prisoner secure." the XO told the Captain of the *Patrick Henry*. "Who is our guest, sir?"

"That's classified as top-secret, but he's obviously a high value cargo. He's someone who our friends at the Agency have been anxious to secure for quite a long time. So tell the Seal team "well done" and then have our navigator plot us a course out of here as quickly as possible. Clear the bridge, secure all hatches and prepare to dive!"

Down in the control room, below the conn deck, the diving officer followed a strict set of procedures. Speed was set to all ahead two-thirds. The last critical hull opening - the main induction tube - was sealed and an array of green lights confirmed that the boat was fully pressurized and secure. Ballast tank vents were opened next to fill with water, thus increasing the sub's diving speed.

"Rig out the bow diving planes and set them on full dive." the Captain ordered. "Make our depth 80 feet."

"Aye, sir, approaching cruising depth. Leveling off and adjusting trim. Ready to accelerate to our normal cruising speed of 25 knots on your command."

"Roger. Make it so."

The *Patrick Henry* was thus fully underway, ready to descend south along the Chilean Pacific coast to the Straits of Magellan; east through it to the Atlantic Ocean; and then up along the Argentine coastline. It was following the normal submarine Blue Route 1 above the deep abyssal plane, paralleling the Mid-Atlantic Ridge as it snaked up towards the Caribbean Sea and to the continental margin of the US east coast beyond. Several days clear running and it would first surface at the world's largest military maritime base, the Norfolk Naval Station in Hampton Roads, Virginia. The majority of the US's nuclear-powered submarine fleet called The Groton Naval Submarine Base in New London, Connecticut, its home port, so this landing at Norfolk would be a special intermediary stop, safely to deliver its high value prisoner to waiting CIA agents. From there he would be whisked off to a black incarceration and enhanced interrogation site near Langley, Virginia.

XI

All seemed to be proceeding to plan, or so the Captain thought. But just as they were passing by the edge of the continental shelf off of the Lesser Antilles, skirting the almost bottomless depths of the Puerto Rican Trench, the Captain was informed by his Sonar Supervisor that, enigmatically, the ship was clearly being followed. An analysis of the engines, hydraulic pumps and screw blade configurations of the pursuers quickly identified them as being that of Russian Yasen Class nuclear-powered attack submarines. Not just one, a pair of them, which were quickly identified as the "*Arkhangelsk*" and the "*Perm*". Fast, agile, and bristling with armaments, they were keeping their distance while remaining clearly locked in on the *Patrick Henry*.

"Why? What could they possibly know about our mission?" the Captain wondered. It was not uncommon to hear of Russian surveillance submarines operating in the international waters off the east coasts of both Central and North America, but they had always maintained a very low, stealth profile and kept their distance. This was certainly unusual and very troubling behavior. Perhaps, the Captain thought, these two subs were on a lethal mission to destroy his ship and its high value cargo?

Before the Seal Team 6 had stormed the *Glasnost* to extract Stern from Russian detention, he had been heavily drugged and subjected to excruciating enhanced interrogation by his captors. They had successfully extracted his remaining vial of Viking sands from him, but they had also coerced him into admitting that there was yet another small cache of the potent weapon hidden in an unidentified location in his Argentine *estancia*. So as long as it remained hidden there with Stern in American hands and willing to show them where this last vial was, the Russians feared a Cold War type standoff involving the mutually assured destruction of each country's remaining trove of their priceless oil resources. Action had to be taken to prevent this, even at the risk of creating an international incident that could lead to an all out war between the world's remaining superpowers. But it would not provoke one if the encounter could be made to look like it had caused an unfortunate and unintended maritime accident. That is what the Russian attack subs had been tasked to do.

XII

"Give me their current range, heading and speed." the Captain ordered.

"Aye, sir. 1,500 meters astern, lying 220 degrees west; proceeding east at 25 knots on a 120 degree heading." the XO replied.

"They seem to be trying to herd us ENE. Verify what's out there in that direction." But the Captain already knew. Skirting perilously through canyons in the foothills of the Mid-Atlantic Ridge, the sub was heading straight towards towering seamounts, both straight ahead and to its starboard side. A devastating collision would be unavoidable if the deadly chase continued at its current course and speed.

"Ping them several times as a warning." the Captain ordered.

"Aye, sir. Our distance to the seamounts is closing fast! Your orders, please?"

The wily old Captain knew exactly what to do next. It would be a maneuver straight out of one of his favorite films, "Top Gun", but in a perilous maritime setting instead.

"Steady on course." he commanded. "On my mark prepare for rapid resurfacing. Blow out the ballast tanks and set the diving planes for emergency ascent! All engines to be set to neutral. 3, 2, 1, Mark!"

The unexpected maneuver caught the two Russian pursuit subs completely by surprise. They had recklessly approached at great speed, seeking to drive the *Patrick Henry* into the looming cliffs of the towering seamounts. Instead they had overshot their mark and were both themselves careening towards certain destruction. Their delicate steering mechanisms had been temporarily overwhelmed by the extreme turbulence that was generated by the *Patrick Henry's* sudden, unexpected change of course. The lead Russian sub, *Arkhangelsk*, was way over-committed. Despite its desperate avoidance efforts it slammed directly into a giant seamount with full and lethal force. It broke in half and sunk immediately into the abyssal depths. Stunned, the *Perm* just barely managed to avoid collision with another huge seamount. It finally came to a complete halt about 50 feet below and slightly ahead of the *Patrick Henry*. Its unprotected position left it perilously exposed to its adversary's full array of armaments.

"Ping them twice again and open a hailing frequency." the Captain told the XO. "Time we had a talk with the remaining crazy Ivan."

"This is Captain Robin Forman of the USN nuclear submarine, Patrick Henry. We regret the unfortunate accident that befell your colleague ship-in-arms. We urge you to surface immediately and institute search and recovery operations for any survivors. We caution you to keep your distance from us and not to impede our further peaceful passage through international waters. Understood? Over."

But the Captain's transmission was predictably met only by radio silence. Turning back to his XO the Captain ordered the hailing frequency to be closed, the sub's depth to be readjusted and a course reset for the Norfolk Naval Station at top cruising speed of 33 knots. Potential international hostilities had been successfully avoided and Albert Stern was securely on his way to a CIA black site for interrogation and debriefing.

PART 3
SABOTAGE AND WAR CLOUDS

"Demoralize the enemy from within by surprise, terror, sabotage and assassination. This is the war of the future."

I

The Russian President had tasked the FSB covertly to take oil production by Nigeria, Venezuela and Angola offline, thus eliminating 7.5 million bbls/day of crude oil from the world's daily supply. It would be done by the selective sabotage of what appeared to be soft and easy targets. After that, Russia's biggest rivals, the Saudis and the Americans, would have to be tackled, but those would be far bigger tasks. For now, the FSB was ready to rise to the initial challenge.

II

Monday, December 3rd, Port Harcourt, Nigeria, 23:00 GMT +1

Colonel Borisenko and Major Fortunatov were back to work sooner than they had expected. The FSB had ordered them to Nigeria to "assist" a diplomatic effort by the Russians to gain favor with Africa's biggest oil producer. Of course they knew that it was all a sham and that their work would be far more sinister. While Russia's formal diplomatic efforts would be cloaked in empathy and aid for Nigeria's struggling economy, their task would be to begin systematic elimination of production by Russia's competitors, starting with

Nigeria's 1.4 million bbls/day. This would be accomplished through secret liaison with the rebel Movement for the Emancipation of the Niger Delta (MEND), still smarting many years later from the ruthless crushing of the Biafra independence initiative in the mid-1960s by the central government. They had set up a meeting with Akin Ateri the next evening, President of the clandestine renegade organization. The situation was ripe for manipulation and the Russians knew it. It would take very little to tip the balance into utter chaos, resulting in their desired shutdown of Nigerian oil exports to the world.

Ateri was very satisfied with recent developments. He had just ordered another successful attack on a major oil export pipeline operated by a local subsidiary of the Italian State oil firm, Eni SpA. Earlier he had publicly promised to resume MEND's deadly assaults against the Nigerian petroleum industry. Now his most recent one had just succeeded dramatically. ENI had lost over 4,000 bbls/day from the damage to its pipeline. The attack had had an immediate panic impact on the scarce global oil supply, sending already stratospheric prices soaring even higher.

Over a period of years Nigeria's oil output had been reduced by 28% due to MEND's relentless deadly attacks on targets like drill sites, pipelines, tankers and oil processing facilities. Kidnappings of key expat personnel of foreign oil companies and bombings of their critical oil installations in the Niger Delta Region had taken their toll as well. MEND's ultimate, sinister plan was to stifle all oil production and to cripple the Nigerian government economically.

Not even an earlier government-sponsored amnesty had weakened or deterred Ateri's iron will to seize control of the Delta's vast oil riches for his long-suffering Urhobo tribesmen. They had languished for too long in poverty and devastating ecological ruin in Niger and Bayelsa states. Regular, uncontrolled spills had been a prominent feature of Nigeria's oil industry since crude was discovered there more than 60 years before. An estimated 240,000 barrels of crude oil were spilled in the Niger Delta every year, polluting waterways, contaminating crops, and releasing toxic chemicals into the air.

Recently a new group, the Niger Delta Avengers (NDA), had emerged on the scene with the same goals as MEND. It too sought to run the oil companies out of the Niger Delta and give those who lived there as much control over oil operations as possible. A working accord was soon established between the two rebel forces. The group was as well-armed as MEND, having at its disposal weapons and materiel ranging from machine guns and speedboats to multi-barreled rocket-launchers. And, like MEND, the NDA has been successful at hitting high-value, strategic targets, such as Shell's Forcados oil pipeline, Chevron's Okan offshore platform and ExxonMobil's Qua Iboe terminal, which was Nigeria's largest. Not surprisingly, their attacks had had the same crippling effect on Nigeria's oil production as those by MEND – a drop of 800,000 bbls/pd from 2.2 to 1.4 million, the lowest production level in 25 years.

III

At the appointed time of 23:00 on a moonless night, Borisenko and Fortunatov waited patiently to be picked up outside of the well-appointed Golden Tulip Port Harcourt Hotel. All was quiet up and down the street but for the occasional thump of tires navigating through the potholes in the empty road. Then, out of the shadows, a Toyota Hilux pickup truck - known as a "technical"- appeared and pulled to a stop in front of them. They could see the barrel of a heavy-duty machine gun just barely poking out from under a tarp in the truck's flatbed.

Prearranged code words were quietly exchanged and two burly, masked, MEND paramilitaries hopped out of the truck and beckoned to the Russians quickly to get in. Fortunatov purposely stumbled on the rough roadway, momentarily to divert the soldiers' attention, while Borisenko secretly slapped a magnetic mini GPS tracker under the splayed rear left fender of the technical as he stepped onboard. Now, wherever they were going, they could be tracked by satellite by both the Russian embassy in Abuja and the FSB's HQ in Moscow. Once inside the obligatory hoods were slipped over their heads, which they had fully expected. No sense objecting. The vehicle would be tracked to its destination anyway.

After a 45 minute drive on rough and dusty roads the technical finally came to an abrupt halt. As their hoods were removed, Borisenko and Fortunatov could see that they had come to a stop inside the driveway of an isolated, ram-shackled villa, much the worse for wear. But when they stepped inside they were quite surprised by the opulent setting. And there, standing in the middle of the great room, surrounded by AK-47 toting guards, was MEND's President, Akin Ateri.

"Gentlemen, welcome!" Ateri greeted them. "Get them some cold Star beers to slake their thirst after such a dusty journey." he ordered one of the guards to do.

"Mr. President,"Borisenko replied, "thank you for agreeing to see us. We believe that we can be of great assistance to your movement."

"Yes, so I have been told. Tell me exactly how so, Colonel?"

"We would like to assist you in taking complete control of oil production from the Niger Delta, as is the right of your long oppressed peoples."

"Interesting, but why would you do that?" Ateri queried. "What's in it for you?"

"Friendship and cooperation." Borisenko replied. "We may no longer be a communist country but our socialist roots still run deep.

We believe in empowering the people whose scarce resources have been plundered from them for far too many years now." None of Ateri's people, though, sensed the extreme irony of the fact that the Russian people in the Siberian producing regions had lived pitifully, from hand-to-mouth, for many years with no share in the profits from their oil resources that had been commandeered by the central government in Moscow.

"And how will you do that?" Ateri asked.

"By helping you destroy the infrastructure that the vampire elite in Abuja have used to steal your oil and sell it abroad at great profit, none of which your people ever see. The sales money goes into the Federation Account at the Central Bank and then secretly into the pockets of your oppressors. This can all be brought to a halt with your cooperation." Borisenko continued. He knew that he was squarely on script now and that Ateri's interest had begun to peak.

Discussions between the two men on a very specific plan of attack went on well into the night. By the early light of dawn Ateri was clearly on board. "Game on!" the Russians thought with great satisfaction.

IV

Back again at the hotel, Borisenko sent a detailed, coded report electronically to FSB Chief Chestnoy in Moscow. It was reviewed and quickly received full approval. The terse reply was "идти - Go!"

"*Arkasha*, what have you arranged with the Chadian mercenaries?" Borisenko asked.

" Everything is in place, Colonel. They will be arriving soon under the guise of being casual workers, hired to help build the supposed infrastructure projects that our official delegation is spuriously offering to finance for the central government."

"Excellent! And where is the map of the Nigerian gathering and export pipeline networks?"

"*Vot*, have a look. The main pipeline hub is at Warri, from where the Trans-Nigeria Pipeline feeds the Lagos area. Then there are branches that connect to the Trans-Saharan and West African pipelines, which are the two main export routes to Algeria and Ghana. If the rebels take out the main complex at Warri, it will shut down all Nigerian internal transit, as well as its profitable exports. That will entirely cripple the Nigerian economy, which relies on its petroleum export earnings for almost all of its government revenues."

"Exactly, *Arkasha*. And it will leave the facilities around Port Harcourt intact, leading MEND to believe that they will have full control of the country's remaining production and export capabilities. Just the plan we needed to sell to them!"

V

At 02:00 on the overcast night of Thursday, December 6th, the Russians waited to meet Ateri and his high level colleagues, this time in the shadows of the vast processing, refining and pipeline hub at Warri. The Chadians had all been employed by NNPC, the Nigerian State oil company, as cheap labor to do routine exterior pipeline maintenance. It had all seemed fully innocuous. But in the process they had carefully placed powerful, shaped plastic explosive charges along key points of the entire oil processing, refining and transport system at the hub, to be simultaneously detonated by remote control. Everything was in place for a massive act of sabotage.

Well out of sight of the skeletal crew of security guards around the sprawling complex, a convoy of MEND and NDA operatives arrived. Everyone wanted to see the ensuing chaos and victory. Ateri himself, flanked by two heavily armed personal guards, stepped out of an armored technical and approached the waiting Russians.

"*Dobre vecher.*" Ateri greeted them in a friendly fashion. "Do you have the detonation device primed for action?"

"Of course, Mr. President. You will have the honor of setting it off."

"Fine, let me direct my executive cadres to get in position to watch the show." At a beckon from Ateri, his closest associates joined him for the viewing. In all, the top echelons of both MEND and NDA, along with many of their rank and file paramilitaries, were assembled to watch the impending disaster.

While Borisenko continued to engage Ateri in conversation, Fortunatov sent an electronic signal to the Chadian mercenaries, who were assembled at a distance out of sight, to be on standby.

"Mr. President, we are ready when you are. Here is the detonating device." Borisenko said. "Type in code 666 and then hit the red button."

Atari eagerly followed the instructions and the ensuing series of explosions were catastrophic. A deafening roar engulfed the entire complex, causing 20 meter high flames to leap up into the night. The critical Warri oil facility was instantaneously in complete ruin.

In the ensuing noise, smoke and chaos, no one at first heard the steady chatter of machine guns. From over 100 yards away, under deep cover, the Chadian mercenaries were systematically mowing down the entire MEND and NDA delegation. Ateri was stunned.

"Who is doing this?" he stammered. "Did someone alert the government troops?"

"No, Mr. President. Sorry about all of this." Borisenko said, smiling wryly as he leveled his FSB OTs-38 silent service revolver and shot Ateri several times through the back of the head. Fortunatov simultaneously dispatched his two bodyguards.

Fleeing the horrific scene in a waiting, unmarked Russian embassy motor pool vehicle, Borisenko and Fortunatov engaged in animated conversation.

"Perfect, Colonel, our mission is accomplished!" Fortunatov gloated. "The government will never know what really happened. Their oil export infrastructure is in total ruins and their rebel adversaries have all been slaughtered. Let them try to figure it out. There is no one left to tell them anyway. But it doesn't really matter at all, does it?"

"*Nyet, Arkasha*." Borisenko replied with huge satisfaction. I will inform Moscow of all of the details. Our work here is successfully done."

VI

Friday, December 7th, The Lubyanka, Moscow, Russia, 10:00 GMT +3

General Chestnoy at the FSB was extremely satisfied with the news he had just received from Nigeria. In a deft stroke, 1.4 million bbls/pd of crude oil had been indefinitely eliminated from the world market. Russia's planned total hegemony over the world's crude oil markets was squarely on its initial course.

"*Misha*," Chestnoy said to his adjunct, Colonel Mikhail Luzhkov, "we are in business! Time to initiate our next step."

"And what will that be, General?"

"Cabinda in Angola. Another 1.37 million bbls/pd to remove from production. This will be a bit more difficult, but we have our assets well assembled. I assume that the Chadian mercenaries were satisfied with their compensation for the Nigerian job?" Chestnoy asked.

"Indeed, General, they can hardly wait to learn of their next assignment."

"Excellent, get in touch with their commandant, Dominique Hadjean, and tell him that we have another very lucrative job for him and his men. Inform him that he must recruit a few Portuguese-speaking lieutenants, but that the rest of his brigade must always remain silent during the course of the operation. And let Borisenko and Fortunatov know that their next mission is imminent."

"конечно, General, it shall be done immediately".

VII

The political situation in Angola had been volatile for many years. Its status has been disputed by many local political organizations, most notably by The Front for the Liberation of the Enclave of Cabinda (FLEC), which had fought for independence for several decades before opting for an uneasy ceasefire. But this oil-rich region continued sporadically and sometimes violently to demand its independence from Angola, claiming it had been marginalized and exploited.

Cabinda, is located 383 KMs north of the capital Luanda. It is an enclave, separated physically from the country's main landmass by a slender finger of the Democratic Republic of Congo's (DRC) territory. It is Angola's smallest province, covering 7,000 km/sq., bordering on the Republic of Congo to the north and the DRC to the east and south. The Cabinda region produces up to 70 percent of Angola's oil revenues that make up half of the country's GDP. The crown jewel of its wealth is the heavily guarded base of Cabinda Gulf Oil Company at Malongo, 12 miles north of Cabinda town. Cabinda Gulf, is a subsidiary of the U.S. oil company Chevron. It produces 55% of Angola's 550,000 bbls/day. Up to 50,000 troops of the Angolan armed forces guard it 24/7.

The plan would be first to create a chaotic diversion by having the Chadian mercenaries attack the Angolan army garrison guarding Cabinda Gulf's base. They would be disguised as FLEC separatist rebels. It would be a silent sneak attack, launched with mortars and artillery in the early morning hours. It wouldn't matter what the ultimate outcome of that battle would be, though, as it was not the main sabotage plan. That would occur under the sea, in Takula, off the coast of Cabinda. It is where several behemoth producing platforms were located, all equipped with the latest technology for deep water drilling and production.

VIII

Friday, December 14th, South Atlantic Ocean off the coast of Cabinda, Angola, 23:30 GMT +1

Running silently at a depth of 60 meters in the very early morning hours, two specially altered Husky class Russian submarines approached the vast complex of subsea wellheads and risers that lay beneath the producing platforms of Cabinda's prolific Takukla offshore oilfield. Amongst the newest of Russian attack class submarines, they had an incredibly low acoustic signature and could deploy advanced technology to operate various varieties of unmanned, automated robotic underwater vehicles (UUVs). Captains Igor Vasiliev of the *"Kursk II"* and Oleg Popov of the *"Petrograd"* were maintaining radio silence between them as they readied their crews for action.

"Activate the UUVs for immediate deployment." Captain Vasiliev ordered. With that the first mate took virtual control of two heavy-duty UUVs as they emerged from their storage compartments at the front of the sub. The same sequence was happening simultaneously aboard the *Petrograd*.

THE VIKING SANDS : ENDGAME

"*Da*, sir, ready to set charges."

"Mine the blowout preventer stacks first and then just above them at the junction with the risers." Vasiliev continued. "Monitor carefully for any enemy sonar detection. We need to be finished and out of here quickly!"

Given the immense pressure and heat generated by the production of petroleum, extensive redundant safety measures needed to have been put in place on each wellhead and riser to prevent a catastrophic blowout, spill and ensuing fire. Mounted atop each wellhead was a blowout preventer stack (BOP) that consisted of a series of massive rams, chokes and kills to control oil flow and to shut it swiftly down in the event of an emergency. When a well is open and flowing at the desired rate though, the oil is transported to the surface of the platform for treatment, storage and tanker loading through flexible 30" diameter, 50 foot "riser" pipes, joined end-to-end. Through these devices and channels an immense amount of volatile crude oil may be flowing at any moment.

Deftly maneuvering the UUVs in minimal subsea light, the technical experts aboard each sub secured shaped plastic explosive charges to key points on the numerous BOP stacks and riser junctions attached to each subsea wellhead.

"Set the timers simultaneously for 30 minutes." Captain Vasiliev ordered. "We will be well clear of the danger zone by then and into much deeper water. Make haste! Ready us to maneuver and dive!"

"*Da*, sir." the XO responded. With that he took control of the sub and initiated propulsion and diving sequences, as the nearby *Petrograd* followed suit. At the appointed, synchronized time the two subs slipped away as the timers ticked down to the forthcoming doomsday scenario. The die for catastrophic destruction was irrevocably cast.

IX

At the Angolan army garrison guarding the Cabinda Gulf Oil compound the battle raged. In the pitch darkness of night the Chadian mercenaries besieged the defenders with artillery, mortars, rockets and blistering machine gun fire. It had been such an unsuspected attack that it took quite a while for the Angolan army units to mobilize. Fatalities on their side were already heavy. The disguised mercenaries showed no mercy.

"Who are they?" the army commander stammered in shock.

"We can't be sure, sir, but they sound like FLEC rebels. I can hear orders and screams from them in Portuguese." his *aide de camp* replied.

"Quick, alert Army Provincial HQ in Cabinda that we are under attack. Also cable the General Staff in Luanda that we are just barely holding on. We need air support and reinforcements immediately!" At that very moment the room shook violently as an artillery shell took off a section of the roof above them.

Outside Commandant Hadjean looked on with satisfaction as his men pinned down the Angolan army defenders in their swiftly deteriorating complex. Then his Apple watch received an anticipated coded message: "Undersea work completed. We are returning to the abyssal depths. Detonation will occur in 5 minutes. Cease all hostilities and disappear into the night. (s) Vasiliev."

And so, to the utter astonishment of the beleaguered Army garrison commander, a sudden silence fell over the battlefield, leaving behind only the smell of gunpowder and death.

X

At exactly 15 minutes after midnight on the morning of December

15th a series of violent explosions erupted undersea at the Takula oilfield complex. Great billows of sulfurous crude oil welled up from the ruptured wellheads and risers and quickly caught fire. The sea was a sudden inferno of flames and ear-splitting explosions. Crews on the production platforms struggled to launch evacuation pods in the growing emergency. Those who jumped off the platform would fall to their certain deaths. Chaos ruled everywhere. Only later, in the bleak light of dawn, would it become apparent that Angola's biggest oil producing area was in complete ruin and that it would be off production for an interminable period.

XI

Removing Venezuela as a competitor would be the easiest of the three sabotage tasks for the Russians. Decades of disastrous Bolivarian Socialist rule had already reduced this once proud, oil-rich nation to being the basket case of the Western Hemisphere. Its once substantial oil production of more than 3 million bbls/day at the beginning of the century had dwindled in the last two decades to 1.4 million bbls/day and more recently to a paltry 0.5 million bbls/day. Ongoing political chaos and severe social unrest in the country now further threatened to reduce or even halt all production by the State oil company, PDVSA. Added to that, new sanctions imposed on Venezuela had eliminated its previously steady export to the US of 400,000 bbls/day. This was a house of cards ripe for both revolution and total collapse. Exactly what the Russians wanted. It wouldn't take much to tip the balance.

The FSB had already identified the easiest targets for catastrophic sabotage. Major oil pipelines brought Venezuela's crude oil production from its mammoth Orinoco Heavy Oil Belt fields to refineries and export facilities at both Puerto Jose and Puerto La

Cruz on the Caribbean Sea. The same was true of its production of heavy Boscan crude, which was piped to similar facilities at Amuay from Venezuela's second largest producing area, Maracaibo Lake. But the very nature of this asphalt-based, non-viscous crude oil would be the crux of Venezuela's catastrophic downfall.

XII

Wednesday, December 19th, The President's Executive Office, the Kremlin, Moscow, Russia, 09:00 GMT +3

Both General Chestnoy and Colonel Luzhkov sat a bit nervously outside the President's office in the Kremlin, waiting to be summoned for their audience with him. They were confident that their operations in both Nigeria and Angola would have pleased the President, but they knew that he still had some questions about their planned sabotage operation in Venezuela. The President was always sharp, incisive and very much to the point.

"The President will see you now. Please follow me." his executive secretary said dispassionately. "He has a very tight schedule this morning, so please be concise and quick."

"*Privyet, Gospodin President.*" Chestnoy began upon entering. But the President was clearly in no mood for small pleasantries. He wanted to get straight down to the matter at hand.

"Tell me, General, how this operation in Venezuela will be conducted. It must be completely beyond detection, of course. We have been very helpful to the failing regime there with both generous loans and technology. They are completely in our debt. How can you assure me that your proposed operation will be both successful and plausibly deniable, if necessary? Better still, completely untraceable?"

"Colonel Luzhkov will explain, sir".

"The inherent weakness in the Venezuelan pipeline system and the nature of the crude oil it carries will be the linchpin of our covert cyber attack, sir." Luzhkov began. "Because of the heavy, non-viscous nature of their crude oil, heat must be applied to guarantee that its viscosity reaches acceptable values for transport in pipelines. Heat loss is always present during oil flow and numerous heating stations must be located along the pipelines to prevent gradual cooling in the line. A project involving heated pipelines is not an easy task. It involves technical considerations regarding pipeline expansion, number and capacity of pumping stations and estimates related to heat loss. In addition it is technically difficult to heat a large oil volume to avoid heat loss during its transit in an oil pipeline. It is quite expensive too, due to the high cost of heat generation."

"And so how does all that advance our objectives?" the President interrupted impatiently.

"Considering the US to be its mortal enemy, sir, the Bolivarian Socialist regime ordered their national oil company, PDVSA, to purchase only Russian oilfield and pipeline technology. We have become a creditor of last resort for the government in Caracas, lending it billions in hard currency as its economy continues to implode. They are very grateful to us, so we are beyond suspicion. Thus it will be both convenient and easily planned to use the unique characteristics of Venezuelan crude that I have described as the Achilles' heel that will cease Venezuelan oil production indefinitely. It's as simple as inserting a sophisticated Trojan horse into our software that PDVSA has been ordering exclusively to use."

"And has that been done already?" the President demanded.

"Yes, sir. They are wholly reliant on our technology. We have been very careful to let them use it successfully for a while, so they should suspect nothing. On your order we will remotely activate it covertly." Luzhkov replied.

"Do it now then! Be sure our tracks are invisible. *Udachi,* but it had better work flawlessly!" With that caveat the President got up and left for his next scheduled meeting with the waiting Inner Politburo.

As Chestnoy and Luzhkov exited the meeting room the former told the latter immediately to contact the cyber warfare sub-unit in the FPI and instruct them to activate the Trojan horse in PDVSA's pipeline software as soon as possible. "First, have them confirm that the particular pipeline to be attacked is full of crude oil in transit to the seacoast. We want as big an explosion and fire as possible. Then, have them wait until a very large batch is arriving at the end of a line so that the destruction will spread throughout the entire refining and export loading complex."

XIII

Friday, December 21st, PDVSA Operational Coordination Control Center, La Salina, Venezuela, 09:00 GMT -4

PDVSA Operational Coordination Control Center in La Salina is charged with absolute authority over the movement of all crude oil through the web of transit pipelines to its refineries, tankers and export shipping terminals. Critically, from there, the Automated Operations Center controls and monitors all pipeline movement of crude oil and natural gas in transit throughout the complex, countrywide system. On this particular day, Supervisor of Pipeline Operations, Luis Martinez, was coordinating the movement of large batches of oil down the pipeline network from the interior oilfields to the tanker loading facilities in the various export ports along the Caribbean coastline.

"Manuel," he asked his assistant, "what is the pressure and temperature in the line to Puerto José?"

"Normal, *Jefe*. 820 psig at 50 degrees C. The batch is moving along without any impediment. Estimated remaining transit time is less than 10 more minutes."

Satisfied, Martinez was about to take a coffee break while the automated system functioned on autopilot when he noticed that an array of unexpected yellow caution lights had suddenly begun blinking on the master control panel. "Manuel, what is the problem?"

"I don't know, *Jefe*. But it seems that both pressure and heat are rapidly building up in the line. I can't explain it. Everything was functioning normally just a few moments ago."

The line could safely contain pressures up to 1,400 psig and heat up to 60 C, but the gauges were already at redline for both of those numbers. Safety countermeasures were initiated to no avail, as the yellow lights all started to turn to critical red. "Shut the line down, Manuel!" Martinez shouted out a desperate order. "Turn off the power to the pumping and heating stations!"

"Too late, *Jefe!*" a frustrated and frightened Manuel replied. "We are already over critical limits and my shutdown command has been rejected."

"*Madre de Dios!*" is the last thing Martinez could remember saying before all hell broke loose.

XIV

Elevated above ground so as to be easily heated, the 30" diameter steel transit pipeline was full to capacity with 90,000 barrels of heavy crude oil when it catastrophically ruptured under intense pressure and high heat. It literally began to fly apart at its seams, being where the welds connected each section of 60' pipe to the next. The extreme pressure and runaway heat initiated by the Trojan horse in the control software were so great that large amounts of superheated, sulfurous oil poured through the numerous breaches in minutes. Almost 420,000 gallons of noxious heavy oil spewed out of the pipeline without warning. In the process of it ripping apart, shards of heated metal filled the air. As sparks flew from the shrapnel of colliding pieces of steel, a fire was quickly ignited. It raged uncontrollably at the rupture point, which was just near the central receiving flange where the web of pipelines arriving from various other producing fields all connected. Resounding explosions soon rent the air, followed instantly by a series of billowing fireballs, each fueled by exploding crude oil pipelines and storage facilities. The result was total destruction of the entire complex at Puerto José, with serious collateral damage to those at Puerto La Cruz. For all intents and purposes, transit of production from Venezuela's largest producing areas would be halted indefinitely.

XV

Thus the Russians had succeeded so far in their initial trifold plan to attain hegemony over the world's crude oil markets. They were very satisfied that their covert sabotage operations had been a complete success to date. Only the Saudis' vast oil reserves and the American's prolific shale and conventional oil production were left to deal with. But they would have to wait for now. The President had also tasked the FSB and the Air and Space Forces with initiating and coordinating an internationally forbidden mission to Mars to obtain more of the devastating Viking sands to be put to nefarious use. The President had hoped that in successfully capturing Stern they would find him with a small but sufficient quantity on his person, but he wanted to be sure of having an ample supply on hand for all future eventualities. So the next facet of the President's master plan would have to be put into motion immediately.

PART 4
CLARITY AND THE COSMOS

"And then it all fell into place."

Thursday, December 27th, CIA Black Site, McLean, VA, 11:30 EST

I

Down a dark, leafy lane, just off Georgetown Pike, sat a rambling old mansion, looking both foreboding and deserted. Gated, with decidedly unkempt grounds, it was rumored amongst McLean schoolchildren to be haunted. Even local hikers heading for the nearby trails through Scott's Run down to the Potomac River gave it a wide berth. And that was just the impression that its anonymous CIA owners wanted to create.

Behind tightly shuttered windows, the interior of the stately old building was a beehive of covert activity. Depending on the nature of its sequestered inmates, it had been retrofitted for either their relentless interrogation or their complete isolation from others seeking to learn of their whereabouts. In the case of the newly arrived inmate, Albert Stern, it would fulfill a delicate mixture of both such functions.

Stern was seated alone on a hard wooden chair in a small, bare room, in front of an empty table. A bright light glared in his eyes. From behind a one-way mirror-glass wall panel Chris Wytham and Dr. Antony Fazio studied him carefully. Fazio was the Agency's chief consulting psychiatrist for enhanced interrogations.

"We haven't been able to crack him at all yet, Tony." Wytham said with great frustration. "He still maintains that he is Alberto Portillo Lopez, who suffered a terrible mountaineering accident but somehow managed to survive. He barely remembers being snatched off the Great Southern Ice Cap by the Russians and even less about our subsequent rescue and his rendition to here. Any memory of his real identity as Albert Stern seems to be completely absent. Is that your diagnosis, Doc?"

"It's hard to tell for certain yet. Clearly he has amnesia, but at first I thought it might only be the transient type, which is self-correcting. The more I speak with him, though, the more I'm convinced that he is in a deep fugue state, suffering from generalized, dissociative amnesia, which is usually permanent. It's a type of mental disorder that involves the total inability to recall important personal information that would not typically be lost to ordinary forgetfulness. It can include a complete loss of one's memory of their identity and life history, which seems to be the case here. It's usually caused by extreme trauma or stress, both of which he has had in abundance in a very short period. Memories of his traumatized self become completely disassociated because they are inconsistent with his everyday functioning self. In short, he really does believe that he is Alberto Portillo Lopez and all memories of his real identity as Albert Stern are deeply suppressed.

"Was it his seeming death plunge to the glacier, Tony? Was that the final trigger for his amnesia?"

"No, Chris, he remembers that in his newly adopted persona. It has to have been the cumulative effects of the unbearable trauma he has caused that finally overwhelmed him and threw him into complete self-denial.

"Whatever it was, it still makes him totally useless to us in his current state of mind." Wytham lamented. "We need to bring him back, debrief him and learn in detail what really happened. Did the

Russians get any of the sands from him? Is there any left that we don't know about? These are all very critical questions! Right now he couldn't even stand trial in his current condition."

"I said that his affliction is usually permanent, Chris, but it isn't always hopelessly incurable. And often, when memories are induced by therapy to return, they do so, suddenly and completely, triggered by something in the victim's surroundings, smell, taste, or a particularly poignant experience. So I have an idea that might bring him back. It's a long shot and it will require very intense cooperation from your Israeli girlfriend, Talia Dagani."

"In my dreams, Tony! We are just professional colleagues." Wytham replied wistfully.

"Well here's your chance to get to know her a lot better. This is what I have in mind...."

II

Talia Dagani was surprised and secretly pleased that Chris Wytham had finally invited her out to dinner. At 20:00 on a Saturday evening he pulled his vintage red 1997 BMW Z3 roadster over to the curb to pick her up at the townhouse in King's Manor, McLean, which was her temporary residence while in northern VA.

"Wow, you look lovely tonight, Talia!" Wytham ventured. Her heady Opium perfume quickly filled the small car with a subtle but delicious scent.

"Why thank you, Chris." she replied engagingly but a bit diffidently. Then they headed down the George Washington Parkway for the Fiola Mare restaurant in DC's upscale Washington Harbor on the Potomac River.

Seated in a small booth overlooking the moonlit river they began with local Chincoteague oysters on the half shell and a glass of chilled Prosecco. The atmosphere was cozy, intimate and filled with budding mutual chemistry. But Wytham knew that he had to get down to business first before he could consider any possible ensuing delights.

"Talia, we need your help. Only you can play the role that could unlock Stern's deeply repressed memory. Please, let me explain."

"Do you always transact Agency business in such lush settings, Chris?" Dagani replied, with a hint of both pique and disappointment in her voice.

"Never before, Talia, but you are very special and this is critical." Wytham went on to explain his plan in detail before they both tucked into sumptuous entrees of whole Dover Sole *Mugnaia* with brown butter and *caper jus*, Meyer lemon and parsley. Then their conversation quickly lightened and became comfortably suggestive as they shared a bottle of Sauvignon Blanc.

On the way back to McLean, along the riverside Parkway, Wytham eased his roadster into one of several overlooks that had an outstanding view of the lights and spires of Georgetown University and the distant DC monuments down the darkened river. He tentatively slid his right arm around Talia's shoulder and caressed her silky soft neck. They drew closer and their lips met in a surprisingly passionate first kiss. Wytham instantly knew then that the rest of the evening would be what he'd been dreaming of for such a very long time!

III

Albert Stern was back in the familiar interrogation room, seated on the same uncomfortable wooden chair. "Another day of relentless questioning." he sighed to himself. But this time, he noticed that the naked light bulb usually glaring in his eyes was slightly deflected so as to afford him a limited view of the dull, featureless room around him.

"Curious." he thought. He had never really seen his interrogators, knowing them only by voice. So he was absolutely astonished when he thought he saw a female form approaching him and then hearing her soft, slightly Middle Eastern accented words.

"Albert, dear, it's me, Leah." she purred, gently taking his cold, clammy hand and stroking the underside of his wrist tenderly. She could feel his pulse racing. "I have missed you so much, but now we can be together again."

Albert was completely perplexed, confused and even panicked. But there was something vaguely familiar about the voice and the distinct aroma of her Opium perfume. His tortured brain was quickly going into overload.

"Leah? Leah who? Do I know you? Why do you seem familiar to me?" he blurted out.

But she had already begun to trigger reactions in him that he could neither explain nor control. Disturbing images of the past flickered dimly before him like ghostly apparitions: the initial explosion in the NASA lab in Houston; the horrendous destruction of the Sterling oil platform in the North Sea; the horror of the nuclear war that he had triggered between Israel and Iran. These were all things that were too unbearable to contemplate and that he had subconsciously suppressed to preserve his fragile sanity.

Calmly a well-coached Talia pursued the ruse. "Of course you know me, dear, we were lovers. Surely you remember?"

Albert struggled mightily to comprehend the utterly confusing moment that he was in. But once again, only vague and tantalizing shadows of things past fleeted through his addled subconscious; wisps of painful, deeply-repressed memories: a vision of the Chamonix aiguilles and the recovery of the cache of Viking sands with Leah; the sudden appearance of the deadly drone, spitting hellfire at them both; Leah shielding him with her body from certain death. Clarity was beginning to emerge....

"But, but...you are dead, Leah!" Albert blurted out. "I remember it all now!"

"No. Albert, it was all staged to look that way." Leah lied convincingly. "It was meant to save you from the lethal intruder and then to take you into protective custody when you descended back down to the parking lot. But you escaped from us then and we have been trying ever since to bring you safely back home."

"Oh, Leah, please save me again!" Stern sobbed, as he desperately clutched her hand.

"You are safe now, Albert." she replied in fake compassion. "Here, have a long drink of water." It was laced with a mild sedative that would ease his shock of traumatic personality re-emergence and lull him into a peaceful and needed sleep.

"Masterful, Tony!" Wytham gasped while watching the whole scene unfold from behind the mirror-glass panel looking into the interrogation room. "It looks like she's done it! We have Stern back!"

Fazio could only nod in complete agreement, flashing a wizened smile at his stunned but grateful colleague.

IV

Tuesday, January 8th, Baikonur Cosmodrome, Kazakhstan, 10:00 GMT +5

The Baikonur Cosmodrome is located 2,100 kilometers southeast of Moscow, on the vast and barren Kazakh steppes. In operation since 1955, the Cosmodrome is one of the Russian Federation's two major space launch complexes. It had been the launch site for Soviet, and later Russian, crewed spaceflights, geostationary satellites and scientific missions to the moon and planets. But today's launch would be for quite a different purpose.

The vehicle processing and launch areas are connected to each other and to the city of Baikonur by 470 km (290 mi) of wide-gauge railroad lines. The rail system is the principal mode of transportation. Rockets are carried from their vehicle assembly buildings to their launch sites horizontally on railcars and vertically elevated onto their pads.

Today's scheduled launch would be of a powerful, un-crewed Soyuz GRAU index 11A511 expendable launch system carrying a moon lander payload. Or so it was maintained publically. But in fact, the moon lander, *Temnaya Luna Kvest (TLK* - "Dark Moon Quest"), was really part of a multi-stage system that would secretly try to launch a lander/soil collector craft, towards Mars from the dark side of the moon. This was strictly forbidden by UN Resolutions, of course. Would the US's surveillance net catch this ruse?

The cover for the Russian plot to reach for and collect the now forbidden sands of Mars was that this was to be a launch not by them, but instead by the Kazakh Space Agency. Kazakhstan had been an independent country since 1991, dating from the time of the breakup of the former Soviet Union. Although there was a total ban on all flights to Mars, carefully monitored launches of communication satellites, other scientific exploration vehicles within Earth orbit and even well defined moon missions by space-capable countries were still allowed. They would be carefully tracked and terminally intercepted by the US's turbo-laser cannon satellite net if they strayed from their flight plans that they had pre-registered with the UN. Russia had advocated hard for permission for their neighbors, the Kazakhs, to explore the dark side of the moon for scientific purposes and to collect samples of that side's uniquely different crust for later examination on Earth. Permission had been granted with a large measure of skepticism. The entire mission would be carefully watched.

Countdown to launch had started the day before and was in its final phases. The huge space vehicle would be inserted into high Earth orbit where the moon lander module would then separate and commence its 2+ day trip to insert itself into a static, geosynchronous orbit above the dark side of the moon. Completely out of view and away from any detection, it would first release the "moon lander", which was completely bogus. It was nothing more than a camera system that would set down on the surface and send back pictures of what would look like the work of a routine scientific survey mission. The real covert purpose of the mission though was still to be deployed.

In the nose cone of the moon orbiting module was yet another spacecraft powered by a revolutionary cold fusion drive that would send it hurtling straight for Mars at such a previously unheard of speed that it would be able to complete a normally year long round trip in no more than 40 days. Designed to the highest standards of stealth technology, it had virtually no radar signature. After the US's surveillance on behalf of the UN began to let down its guard, the craft would be propelled in the darkest hours towards Mars before any countermeasures could be taken against it. Done right, it might never be detected at all. All that was needed was the right window of opportunity to initiate the secret launch. As Czarist General Kutusov said in Tolstoy's War and Peace while he was defending Moscow against the predations of Napoleon's invading army, "The two most powerful warriors are patience and time."

"5, 4, the main engines ignited; 3, tethering bolts released; 2, 1, LIFTOFF!" Rising on a column of fire at one mile a second, the rocket self-corrected its downrange orientation and quickly broke free of Earth's gravity. In just over 5 minutes time it was successfully in high Earth orbit.

So far all had gone perfectly for the Russian's daring plot. But they couldn't have taken into account what Kazakh Assistant Mission Controller, Murat Ibrayev, knew and to whom he might disclose it for profit. In a risky world everything and everyone had a price.

V

Wednesday, January 16th, Oval Office, The White House, Washington, DC, 11:00 EST

Amidst the papers and reports lying in an untidy pile on the President's Resolute desk was NASA's report on the recent moon launch from the Baikonur Cosmodrome. While it was a classified document, it had only been marked "Confidential", denoting the lowest order of secrecy. But this was all about to change.

The President, for his part, hadn't read any of the stack of documents, preferring instead to receive short oral briefings, at least for as long as his ADHD-limited attention span lasted. Thoroughly unorthodox, he often shunned reading even "Top Secret" briefing notes, relying instead on his instinct and "gut" to make critical decisions, often without a grasp of even the basic facts. This morning he was particularly distracted by his usual binge watching of Fox cable news and his irrelevant Twitter fights with an array of perceived antagonists. Although he had stayed in the residence for extended "executive time" that morning, he still wasn't completely ready to engage with the difficult matters of governance confronting him. So he reacted with both annoyance and surprise when his beleaguered Chief of Staff, John Ronin, entered the Oval office unexpectedly, accompanied by CIA Director Baker.

"Excuse us, Mr. President, but have you read the NASA report yet on the scientific moon mission launched from Kazakhstan early last week?" Ronin asked.

"No, not yet. Why?"

"We have reliable information from an embedded covert source that it is a ruse. It is really meant to send a landing craft at hyper-speed from the far side of the moon to Mars to collect more of the oil-destroying sands."

"But isn't that forbidden by UN Resolutions or something? Aren't we supposed to police such things? Our great Space Force can take it out with their high intensity laser cannons. Why wasn't the order to do so given already?" a peeved President reacted.

"It was too late, sir. The spacecraft is already on its way to Mars, well out of range of our satellite weapon net." Baker replied. "Our only hope is to get it when it returns."

"We damn well better then! Incompetence all around me!" the President blurted, his face reddening. "I will talk to the Russian President about this!"

Both men hoped that he wouldn't!

VI

Forty days later *TLK* had completed its forbidden mission to Mars. It had been carefully programmed to avoid detection while on the Martian surface by US surveillance satellites mapping and surveying the red planet from their various low-orbital positions. Both the craft's landing and return maneuvers had been timed to take maximum advantage of the known blind spots in those satellites' planetary scanning patterns. With its sealed hold full of rich, red Martian soil, the craft had successfully blasted off from the surface of the planet and inserted itself into a pre-programmed Hohman transfer orbit back towards its origin point on the dark side of the moon. As far as the Russians knew, their moon mission ruse was still intact.

Traveling at unprecedented speed, *TLK* successfully navigated its way through the perilous asteroid belt between Mars and Earth and then slowed to orbital insertion speed as it approached the moon on its dark side. Here it would re-establish a geosynchronous orbit above the back side of the moon while remaining invisible to any observers on Earth.

Using highly sophisticated telemetry, it would initiate contact with the moon lander that was ostensibly conducting scientific research on the surface. Their two systems would then be synchronized in such a way as to make it appear that the spacecraft that would soon return to Earth was the latter, not the former. All had been carefully planned to make the entire endeavor appear to comply with the UN Resolutions strictly regulating permitted space missions.

At what would be the dead of night in North America the orbiting spacecraft fired its thrusters to break free of the moon's gravity. Simultaneously, on the surface, the lunar lander completely self-destructed, leaving no trace of itself. In this way it would appear that the orbiting rogue spacecraft was actually the lander returning to Earth from its peaceful scientific mission. The die was cast.

VII

Sunday, February 17th, NORAD War Room, Cheyenne Mountain, Colorado, 03:00 MST

NORAD never sleeps. Its surveillance for airborne and space-based threats is always 24/7. Nothing slips past its comprehensive net, especially if it had been tipped off in advance.

Major Andrew Lowen sat tensely hunched in front of his large screen desktop. His hands were cold and even in the air-conditioned control room beads of sweat ran continuously down his face and neck. Brigadier General Lee Weathers, in command of the *TLK* "kill operation", watched intently over Lowen's left shoulder.

The UN Resolution that banned all future flights to Mars was to be rigorously enforced by the US using its net of orbiting X37-B space vehicles armed with powerful laser cannons to annihilate any spacecraft traveling to or from Mars. But their efficacy for such a task had never been tested. No one had ever dared to challenge them. This would be the net's first real-time action.

The safety assumption for the returning Kazakh/Russian scientific mission from, ostensibly, the dark side of the moon was that the US had never tipped the Russians off that it knew its real purpose. While the hyper-speed Mars lander had been duly observed and tracked as it sped away, no attempt had been made to destroy it, as it was already well out of range. It was to be dealt with decisively upon its return.

The Russians felt secure in that no hostile action had been taken after the spacecraft's launch and that a significant amount of time had now passed so as to render it all a backburner matter. Their subterfuge had been masterful, or so they hoped. But they hadn't considered that critical information on the mission could have been leaked to the Americans by a Kazakh dissident seeking both money and asylum.

TLK was less than a few minutes away from the top of the Earth's atmosphere. It appeared to be on a correct trajectory for re-entry. It was programmed to orbit Earth several times while slowly decelerating. Then it would begin a controlled, drogue parachute-assisted, ballistic plunge earthward, to its predetermined touch down point on the vast and empty Kazakh steppes.

THE VIKING SANDS : ENDGAME

"Show me its projected course fast." Weathers commanded. Lowen brought up the space-based image of the fast approaching target on his screen.

"Speed?" Weathers asked.

"17,500 mph, sir." Lowen replied.

"Have the X37-B's laser cannons activated and plot a firing solution. At least 3 of the firing platforms must be synchronized immediately to triangulate on the target."

"Yes sir. Plotting a firing solution. It's tricky, though, as this is such a rapidly moving target."

Weathers sighed deeply. "In fact, that's the least of our problems. This could precipitate a real international crisis! If we destroy the Russian-controlled Kazakh spacecraft they will surely complain to the UN that we have violated our strict policing mandate. They have maintained from the start that it was only a peaceful, information and sample-gathering mission to the dark side of the moon. We would have to disclose our covert information and compromise our sources and methods. We have to inform our superiors of the grave danger immediately. I'm going to call both the Secretary of Defense and the Director of the CIA right away."

"No time, sir. The target is too close to entering the top of our atmosphere and it will be lost in a fiery ball of friction as it begins its descent. The accuracy of our lasers can't be guaranteed under such conditions."

"OK, then, this will have to be on my head. Target acquired?"

"Ready to fire three laser cannons, sir."

Unbeknownst to NORAD, though, the Russians had taken some very specific precautions in advance against such an easy kill. Banks of supercomputers in the city of Vladimir on the Golden Ring, east of Moscow, sprang to life to activate their potent uplink-jamming network, Tirada-2. This highly sophisticated electronic warfare system operated as a mobile complex, normally for the radio-electronic destruction of various enemy command and communication satellites. It could completely overwhelm the protection systems of such satellites, forcing them to spend all of their electrical power on trying to counter Tirada-2's jamming signals. Critically, this would rob them of their ability to receive and carry out command signals from the ground. Acting on instructions from a central control point in Moscow, these mobile units could be moved rapidly to optimal locations from where they could calculate the azimuth and elevation of targets and jam their communications completely. Tirade-2 was a formidable cyber warfare weapon.

"Calibrate and activate the lasers to full power. Concentrate their force on the spacecraft's re-entry heat shield so that the atmosphere can conveniently destroy it. All cannons fire!" Weathers commanded.

"Target acquired, sir. Firing now!"

The directed-energy laser cannons shot searing hot pinpoint beams of 300 KW focused light directly at the approaching spacecraft. *TLK* had no built-in defenses against them. It wasn't at all maneuverable; just very fast. It clearly needed help from Russian electronic ground resources if it had any hope at all of survival.

"We've had a sudden power loss to the lasers, sir." Lowen unexpectedly exclaimed. "We are being heavily jammed by ground based systems in Russia. We can't mount enough juice to get clear shots! We need countermeasures fast!"

Immediately the US Space Force HQ'd at the Redstone Arsenal in Huntsville, Alabama, moved to deploy its satellite based downlink-jamming systems to try to counteract the effects of Tirade-2. Its newly purchased, state-of-the art AIM+ system began continuously scanning Tirade-2's outgoing signals to identify it as the interfering party. Once its mobile units' locations were acquired by GPS, it deployed sophisticated algorithms to digitally process and suppress their transmissions. A battle royal of cyber warfare raged between the ground and low Earth orbit.

"The lasers are powering back up, sir." Lowen hastily informed Weathers. "We are now firing a series of bursts from all three of them."

It was a frantic race against time for *TLK*. Owing to its great speed and miniscule radar profile, it was a very hard target to hit. Repeated bursts of errant laser cannon fire failed to have inflicted any serious damage on it so far. But to enter the atmosphere it had to slow down and flip itself over 180 degrees to expose its heat shield toward the Earth. As it did so several laser beams raked the bottom of the craft inflicting severe damage on the special thermal protection tiles lining its lower surface. They were *TLK's* only safeguard against the searing 3,000 degree Fahrenheit inferno of re-entry. The spacecraft was fatally doomed. Enveloped in a fireball of tremendous friction, it mostly disintegrated as it plunged at terminal velocity to its ultimate demise.

Days later on the winter-frozen Kazahk steppe, a group of nomads who were herding their domestic animals came across the seared and mangled remains of *TLK*. It was just bits and pieces in a shallow crater. They had no idea as to what it was, but amongst the scattered wreckage they noticed a badly charred, sealed canister, still intact. Thinking it might have some value to them as very poor people, they took it and loaded it into a travel bag slung on the side of one of their camels. They wouldn't tell the local authorities of their find, though, for fear of reprisals. But had they escaped from the view of ever-present international eyes carrying out surveillance from space?

VIII

The Russian President was furious at the destruction of *TLK* at the hands of the Americans. He was already incensed at their brazen snatching of Albert Stern right out of their grasp, although, of course, he could never let on that he knew it had ever happened. But within his own internal political fiefdom, someone would have to pay for the spacecraft's loss due to what he assumed to be gross incompetence.

The Russian Supervisor of the Kazakh space mission cowered before the angry President.

"How did this happen?" the President demanded.

Pale white with fear and dread, the Supervisor tried to explain. "It was all kept heavily top-secret, sir. Only a very few persons were fully informed of the mission's real purpose, on a strictly need-to-know basis. The only possibility is that we had a defector betray us. Surely it could not have been a fellow Russian, but there were a few Kazakhs necessarily in the critical knowledge loop. You know that they are very ambivalent about us at best. The FSB is interrogating them all now to ferret out and to deal with whomever it might have been."

"You needn't be personally concerned about it any further." the President replied. "I've ordered that your *propiska* to remain in Moscow be revoked. You are to be transferred immediately to the Mishelevka Radar Station, in Irkutsk."

"But that's in Siberia, sir!" the Supervisor gasped.

"Exactly." came the President's ice-cold reply.

IX

Tuesday, February 19th, Almaty International Airport, Almaty, Kazakhstan, 08:00 GMT +6

Almaty International Airport is the major international departure venue from Kazakhstan. Flights from there connect to most destinations worldwide. It is a busy, crowded and noisy international hub.

On this bright but frigid morning Kazakh citizen, Murat Ibrayev, had come to board an Air Astana flight to Frankfurt, Germany, where he would then transfer on to United's flight 933 to Washington, DC. He had just barely managed to evade the FSB interrogators. He had received his one-way ticket anonymously from a clandestine source in the US, as part of his wealth and asylum deal for having been a useful informant. His new handlers in Langley looked forward to debriefing him further on the state of Russian space technology, their satellite cyber warfare capabilities and any further illicit missions they may have planned.

Ibrayev passed by the crowded Economy Class line and headed straight for the Business Class check-in desk. His large suitcase was awkward to handle as he navigated his way through jostling crowds. Avoiding contact with others was very difficult in the crush of so many unruly people.

But suddenly a large Central Asian man leaning on a metal walking stick slammed into him. It appeared accidental, as the man was quick to make his apologies. Ibrayev hardly felt the prick in his calf as the man's specially adapted assassin's tool fired a tiny pellet into him containing the deadly, fast-acting poison, ricin. Within moments Ibrayev fell dead on the airport floor and no one there knew why.

PART 5
SAUDI APOCALYPSE

"It will come with smoke and the rising of the sun from the west."

I

Monday, February 25th, Dacha Novo-Ogaryevo, West of Moscow, 18:00 GMT +3

This is the place that the Russian President called home. It was built in the 19th century for Grand Duke Sergei Alexandrovich, the brother of Emperor Alexander III. Located on a large, secluded, wooded tract, it was the ideal place for him to escape the frenzied daily political scene in the Kremlin.

It had been unusually cold in Russia this year, exacerbated by the rapidly intensifying nuclear winter that was gripping most of the northern hemisphere in its icy fingers. The stately old mansion was completely surrounded by massive drifts of newly fallen snow. Down a long, tree-lined driveway, constantly being plowed, a small motorcade of Zil and Chaika official limousines made their way towards the residence. All of the President's top confidantes had been summoned once again to an extraordinary meeting of the Inner Politburo.

Inside, before a mammoth roaring fire in the main reception room, sat tables laden with a variety of tasty *zakuskis* and an ample supply of chilled Stolichnaya Kristall vodka. The President greeted his guests and bid them sample the tasty fare. But it wasn't meant to be just a social gathering. The time had finally come to move decisively on with the President's plans for world economic hegemony and domination.

"*Kollegi*," the President began, "now we will start to implement our most difficult but rewarding work. The two biggest targets are within our sights – the Saudis and the Americans. We will move against the former first."

As the assembled guests settled into seats before the fire relishing their plates heavily laden with delectable finger food, the President walked over to a large portrait of Lenin and swung it aside on its hinges to reveal a stout safe built into the wall behind it. He opened it and brought out a small, lacquer palekh box, ornately painted with the scowling continence of Tsar Ivan *Grozny*. From inside he withdrew a thin vial of rust red sand.

"This is what we got from the American pig before he was snatched away from us. We believe that it is all that is left on Earth of the formidable weapon from Mars. It's precious little, so it must be deployed perfectly. *Vanya*," he said to FSB Chief Chestnoy, "you are to devise a plan to destroy the Saudi's largest oilfield and support installations with a portion of it. But you must not leave any traces of our involvement! The rest of it will be used to take down the Americans."

"*Da, Gospodin President*, but this will be very hard. The Saudis certainly won't deal directly with us on any pretense and they are constantly on alert for covert operations menacing their precious national oil patrimony. We must find a trusted, third party interlocutor whom they won't suspect. Perhaps our old friends in the former East German Stasi, posing as oilfield IT engineers? The Germans have considerable expertise about the SCADA system control technology that Saudi Aramco is anxious to install. They developed it. Let me give this some careful thought."

Turning next to his Defense Minister the President sounded a stern warning. "Everything has gone well to plan so far but be very wary of external threats to our national security. Our sometimes allies, the Chinese, are most restive about their ever-dwindling oil supplies. They are beginning to act both desperately and belligerently. We must watch them carefully!" But the President had no clear inkling yet how prescient his concerns really were.

Lastly, the President ordered General Konstantin Volkov, Chief Commander of the Russian Armed Forces, to mobilize all troops of the Joint Strategic Command East both to guard and to fortify the long border with China along the Amur River. "If the Chinese ever decide to move against our vast oil resources in eastern Siberia, it will surely be there." he said. Once again, though, while the President's assumption was reasonable, it could also be fatally off the mark.

Strategic business satisfactorily concluded, the group relaxed into celebratory chatter, reminiscences, toasts and consumption of copious amounts of vodka. All seemed well and on course to them for the President's master plan. The *Rus* would soon be in the ascendancy once again after years of having endured humiliating marginalization.

II

Wednesday, February 27th, US Department of Energy, Washington, DC 11:00 EST

Secretary of Energy, Andrew Finlay, had just returned from a weekly Cabinet meeting at the White House. The discussions, chaired by the attention deficit-ridden President, had been characteristically shallow and often almost irrelevant. But one matter that had received only scant attention had troubled Finlay seriously.

The Secretary of State had tried to brief the President on the successful rendition of Albert Stern back to the US and the national security significance thereof. He expressed great pleasure at the CIA's well-executed covert operation, but at the same time he tried to sound a warning note about the absence in Stern's possession of any further quantities, however small, of the destructive Viking sands. He emphasized that any such remaining quantities were now in the hands of the Russians, who could use them catastrophically.

But the President showed little interest or understanding of the threat that such a situation posed. The National Security Adviser tried to explain the huge risk inherent in what the Russians might do next, but the President preferred to discuss his strategy for the forthcoming mid-term elections instead.

"This could quickly lead to yet another international oil disaster." the Secretary told his Deputy in confidence. "The Russians could easily target us or the Saudis next."

"Clearly, sir. It's more likely the Saudis first, as the Russians know that we know that they have a quantity of the destructive sands. Their plausibly deniable but apparent acts of sabotage in Nigeria, Angola and Venezuela have made their intentions very clear. We should quietly warn the Saudis immediately and increase the vigilance level around our own strategic oil infrastructure to 4.1 Severe - Red."

" I agree, but the President didn't really seem to care. Worse yet if we recommend it, he'll want to do it personally by phone to the King and the Crown Prince. What a mess he'd make of that!"

"The Saudis have the highest levels of security and vigilance already in place, sir. They may thank us politely, but would they heed us at all?"

"A good question," Finlay mused, "but we must at least try."

III

Sunday, March 3rd, Kempinski Al Othman Hotel, Khobar, Saudi Arabia, 23:00 GMT +2

Two German engineers had come from Olpipeline-Telemetrie Dienstleistunger A.G. in Lingen, GDR, where Smart PIGs had been developed. Their mission was both to calibrate the PIGs and to run tests on the new Saudi pipeline SCADA command and control system. It was getting late and the two had eaten and drank much too well. Both were ready to turn in for the night. Their next few days would be long ones, meeting with Saudi Aramco engineers and IT personnel to complete testing and then final commissioning of the sophisticated new monitoring system. So they hadn't noticed the two men sitting across the room nursing their drinks and watching them intently but unobtrusively.

Their observers, Hans Augstell and Reinhart Bandelin from Leipzig, were indeed German IT petroleum engineers as well, but they were also former members of the GDR's infamous and clandestine Stasi "death squads". They had been purposely selected, as they had never been "outed" during the chaotic dissolution of the GDR. They had participated, though, in dozens of assassinations of enemies of the former East German communist regime during the Cold War. Both had been extensively trained for their current assignment by both the FSB and the Russian State pipeline monopoly, Transneft. They were to be handsomely paid if their mission succeeded. Already in their possession were expertly counterfeited German passports and other forged credentials of the two engineers from the real consulting firm in Lingen.

The two engineers rose a bit unsteadily and headed for the elevator bank. So, too, did the two East Germans. As they both got into the lift they exchanged polite greetings. They had each pressed the button for floor 5, and laughed at the coincidence. But it had all been meticulously planned in advance. Augstell tried some chit-chat in German while Bandelin, seemingly engrossed with his iPhone, sent a text to Russian operatives waiting in an unmarked rental van in the back alley to tell them that their plan was a "Go".

"*Gute Nacht, meine Herren.*" Augstell said, as they each turned towards their suites. The East Germans had purposely reserved the suite directly across from that of the real German engineers. Earlier, Bandelin had disabled the hall security cameras to assure complete privacy.

With their backs to the East Germans, the engineers were easy prey. Augstell and Bandelin were both tall and burly. They towered over the unsuspecting engineers as they deftly slipped wire garrots around each of their necks from behind and tightened them mercilessly. Some desperate gurgling and the dastardly deeds were done. It was bloodless and efficient, just as they had been trained.

"Where are the Russians?" Bandelin asked nervously, propping up the dead men as Augstell opened their own suite's door.

"Coming right now." Augstell replied, helping Bandelin drag the corpses inside. From down the corridor three Russian FSB agents exited from the emergency stairwell and hurried to assist the East Germans. It had all happened so quickly, quietly and completely unobserved.

"What will you do with their bodies?" Bandelin asked.

"We will dispose of them using the 'Saudi method'." the lead FSB agent laughed. "Help us move their bodies to our waiting van. By the time they are officially reported as missing you will have completed your job with Saudi Aramco and will be safely back in Leipzig. There will be no trace left of them ever to raise suspicions of foul play!"

IV

Monday, March 4th, HQ of Saudi Aramco, Dhahran, Saudi Arabia, 9:00, GMT +2

Saudi Aramco had just expanded its already massive oil pipeline system covering transport of crude from its numerous producing fields through its processing facilities to its vast export terminal at Ras Tanura on the Gulf. The expansion had required a major upgrade of sophisticated control and monitoring systems along all of the main trunk lines. Thus Aramco's chief technical staff were happy to host the German consultants who would instruct them on the operation of the state-of-the-art SCADA command and control system that they had just purchased.

"*As-salaamu Alaikum*, gentlemen, welcome to our technical support headquarters." Chief Engineer Ibrahim Saad said.

"*Wa-alaikum As-salaam.*" Augstell politely replied.

"We trust that you had an easy trip here and that you are comfortable in your hotel?"

"Quite so." Bandelin replied. "Thank you for your generous hospitality."

"Most assuredly! Let's begin. Brief us, please, on the new software and hardware that we have had installed so that we can start running tests. We are anxious to see how it all improves performance." Saad continued.

"Of course," Augstell replied, "we can demonstrate it all for you over the next few days. Installation is complete and it's just a matter of getting you all familiar with operating the upgrades to your system."

Augstell went on to explain in detail the various components and operating procedures for the new system. In particular he concentrated on the role of the 3,800 lb., fourth generation, specially designed Smart PIGs that would collect, analyze and transmit continuous data as they traveled through the pipelines. They would be linked through the SCADA system to the world's GPS satellite network so that they could provide moment-to-moment telemetry reports on movement of oil batches through the pipelines, while measuring, as well, any corrosion, wear and any other such damage. Russian Transneft had purchased some Smart PIGs for its own vast oil and gas pipeline networks. Thus the East German engineers' employers were already thoroughly familiar with both the PIG's operation and, unspokenly, with its deadly potential as a weapon of catastrophic destruction.

Hidden from the Saudis by Augstell was the fact that one particular Smart PIG that had been designed to run the main 36" pipeline from Ghawar to Abqaiq to Ras Tanura had been fitted undetectably with a horrific doomsday weapon. In a sealed and invisible compartment in its pointed nose was a portion of the remaining Viking sands - about the same amount that had completely destroyed the UK's Sterling oilfield. They would be released in a violent collision triggered by an overriding command relayed to the PIG by a seemingly harmless weather satellite, in low Earth orbit, as it passed over Saudi Arabia. The command would originate in Moscow, but through a series of deft jumps through vulnerable IP addresses in a variety of countries, it would ultimately appear to have come from Yemen, where a Saudi led coalition had been pounding the Houthi rebels with air strikes for almost 8 years. This would further confuse the beleaguered Saudis, if they ever recovered from the initial shock of the forthcoming catastrophic devastation.

During the next few days numerous Smart PIGs of various dimensions were programmed into the Saudi Aramco SCADA system and tested through the vast web of crude and product pipelines covering the Kingdom's principal oil producing and exporting regions. These continuous and repetitive drills would assure that all would go as nefariously planned on the appointed day. Asked if they could stay for the official commissioning ceremony of the new system, Augstell and Bandelin expressed their sincere regrets due to pressures of urgent business waiting for them in Lingen.

V

Thursday, March 7th, Ghawar Oilfield Pipeline Terminus, Eastern Province, Saudi Arabia, 7:00, GMT +2

The incoming Smart PIG from the intermediate oil pipeline station at the Abqaiq processing facility was due to arrive exactly on time at the feeder flanges connecting the pipeline to the northern end of the sprawling Ghawar oilfield complex. This news was greeted with great satisfaction by the Saudi Aramco management team that had come from Dhahran to witness the conclusion of its initial transit along the principal crude oil export pipeline from Ras Tanura. It was a clear validation of the expensive new SCADA signaling and control technology that had just been successfully certified by the bogus German engineers, who had now returned to their home in Leipzig.

"Expensive and complicated, but clearly worth it." Chief Engineer Saad remarked to his distinguished visitors. "We now have meter-by-meter control and continuous readouts of oil volumes flowing through the entire pipeline system. It is marvelous new technology!" he enthused.

At the complex control board all lights were initially flashing green. But then, suddenly, everything changed inexplicably! Previously stable telemetry readouts started fluctuating wildly. There was a clear indication of an out of control emergency occurring. The massive Smart PIG had suddenly begun to hurtle towards its final destination at a recklessly uncontrollable rate of speed. It slammed into the terminus of the pipeline with the accumulated energy of a small, tactical nuclear device, scoring a direct hit on the very center of the junction of the vast tank farm complex with the main feeder pipeline from the Ghawar oilfield. A resounding explosion rent the still air, followed instantly by a series of billowing fireballs, each fueled by exploding crude oil storage tanks. That was horrific enough for the assembled dignitaries to see, but what happened next was completely beyond their ability to comprehend.

As the continuing explosions rocked the center of the complex, they suddenly paled in comparison to the immense blue-white aura that erupted high into the sky and began to engulf the entire terminal. Crackling with searing heat and static electricity like a monstrous tempest, it rolled out from the center of the complex, directly towards the terrified observers. Preceding it there had been an ear-splitting crash and a massive shock wave traveling at lightning speed that was destroying all before it as it went. No one could have known this in the initial turmoil, but the path of the aura's unstoppable force traced the web of pipelines leading from the terminal back to the oilfield that fed them. The Viking sands that had been loosed from the PIG's disintegrated hold were proceeding methodically in their path of destruction down the main pipeline towards the very heart of Saudi Arabia's largest oilfield. In a matter of minutes they would entirely devour most of the proven 59 billion barrels of crude oil reserves that was the vast Ghawar field, the crown jewel of the Saudi's petro-wealth and power.

The control complex's HQ was completely leveled by the shock wave with many lives instantly lost. Luckily, Saad had survived, but he was badly battered, bleeding and dazed, and in a complete state of shock. His entire world had been destroyed in a fleeting instant, right before his unbelieving eyes. Nothing remained now of the complex but grim, charred wreckage strewn all about.

Barely conscious, Saad fumbled in his pocket for his cell phone. He at least had to try to notify Aramco's top management at its HQ in Dhahran of the unspeakable horror that had just unfolded in front of him. But they already knew. They too had heard both the ear-splitting explosion and had seen the same immense, blue-white aura erupting high into the southwestern sky that early morning jogger, Jack Samson, had also incredulously witnessed from Dhahran. The utter carnage inflicted on the Saudi oil infrastructure would be such that it would assure their production would be offline for a very long time, just as the Russians had planned.

PART 6
THE US STRATEGIC PETROLEUM RESERVE

"Deception may give us what we want for the present, but it will always take it away in the end."

I

The Strategic Petroleum Reserve (SRP) is the US's fail-safe, emergency reserve of crude oil. Held under the auspices of the Department of Energy, it is meant to provide a buffer against future world oil supply disruptions. In the perilous world energy environment the US now found itself, it couldn't have been more critically relevant.

The reserve is stored in four natural, underground salt dome caverns in Louisiana and Texas, along the coast of the Gulf of Mexico. Its capacity is 797 million barrels and it is currently full. A series of pipelines link the 4 storage sites both together and to major petrochemical, processing and refining facilities nearby. It is also well connected to the intricate web of trunk pipelines supplying crude oil and product to most regions of the country. In the event of a national emergency, drawdown can be effectuated quickly and efficiently. The entire complex is controlled from the SPR Management Office in Elmwood, Louisiana, near New Orleans.

II

Wednesday, March 13th, The Lubyanka, Moscow, Russia, 09:00 GMT +3

General Chestnoy was sitting with furrowed brow before his large oak desk, deep in thought. An intense man in his mid-70s, his bushy black eyebrows and Stalinesque mustache set off the moon face of a tired old warrior who had seen much over his illustrious career in espionage. On the portly side, his body displayed the telltale effects of too much tension and many too many bottles of vodka over the years. He had ordered not to be interrupted, but the unexpected arrival of his adjunct, Colonel Mikhail Lukhzov, was a welcome exception.

"What's troubling you, General?" Lukhzov asked.

"Ah, *Misha*, good to see you. We have a lot to discuss. The President has set us our most difficult task yet and I am struggling with how to even begin to carry it out. Without giving us much credit for our previous successes, he now wants us to take out the American oil reserves. That would finally leave us as the only significant, fully operational oil producer left in the world. It would be the capstone of his master plan for world economic domination."

"Mmm, a strike against the Americans? I believe it will be very hard, but not impossible to accomplish."

"Indeed, their territory is so vast, almost like ours, and their producing oil areas are scattered widely. I can't think of where we could deliver a decisive blow. But the President is irrationally furious with them after they snatched Stern from us and then destroyed our Mars mission. Still, disrupting the Americans is a core part of his master plan to achieve complete oil domination, so we must think of something viable fast."

"I have been thinking about it too and I may have an idea." Lukhzov replied. " Are you familiar with their Strategic Petroleum Reserve? More than three-quarters of a billion barrels of crude oil, all conveniently stored in interlinked, underground locations. It's perhaps the biggest single oil 'deposit' in the US. And the reserve is connected to all of the major transport pipelines serving their entire country. What a tempting target, General!"

"Interesting, *Misha*, but we wouldn't be dealing with such an easy target as were those in Nigeria, Angola and Venezuela. This is the world's richest and most developed country."

"Granted, but it is now in its own form of political turmoil. The population is deeply and bitterly divided. Over half of them mindlessly support our President's stooge in the White House, who still has some time left in his term. The far right side of his base is reckless and violent. They have openly advocated insurrection, anarchy and destruction of state property. The Reserve is located in what they call "red" states, which are ripe for violence and sabotage. Surely we can find some co-conspirators who would do our bidding for money and political gain?"

"We do have sleeper cells there with agents under our close supervision. But do we have anyone who would know what to do? And would such a person be willing?"

"As we have already seen, General, everyone has their price. Let me do some deep research on our available assets there and then I'll have our staff devise a preliminary plan of attack."

"Agreed, *Misha.* Get back to me as soon as possible!"

III

Times had been very tough for the aging Armand Boudreaux, a Cajun oil worker who provided occasional, routine maintenance to the vast SPR complex. The entire Gulf oil sector had been slowly falling into serious decline. And with new, automated drilling technologies increasingly in use, less and less high-paying, manual jobs were available on the offshore oil platforms that dotted the horizon. As Boudreaux approached what would normally be a well-earned retirement, he was having serious trouble paying his remaining mortgage, feeding his family and providing for their mounting medical costs. He hadn't expected life to be so desperate in his approaching "golden years."

Thus Boudreaux had no choice but to become a socially active political agitator. His former labor affiliation, The Oil, Chemical and Atomic Workers International Union, had provided him with some benefits, but when it merged into a larger conglomerate union, people like him lost both their collective voices and social protections. Increasingly desperate, he had become radicalized by socialist and anarchist dogma, so readily available on the internet. In short, he was just the kind of person that the FSB was anxious to speak with.

There was an advocacy group of people sharing his plight that met weekly in the backroom of The Olde Alehouse, a sleazy dockside saloon. Lots of beer lubricated their hateful rhetoric. Boudreaux thought it was just a place to vent, but in reality, it was well populated by sleeper cell members that the FSB had carefully selected and planted in their midst. They were there to recruit new cell members.

"*Cher* Armand," fellow member Lev Petrov greeted him, "how is it going?"

"Not well." Boudreaux replied disconsolately. "I am almost out of any resources to care for my family. How about you, *mon ami*?"

"Not very good for me either. I get occasional roughneck gigs on offshore oilrigs, but far less often. Two weeks on, two weeks off. Good money, but nothing very steady. It seems that shale oil production has overtaken the offshore as our national market's staple domestic source. What do you do in the industry?"

" I have a casual maintenance job with the SRP. We test it regularly and move cargoes of oil around the four sites to keep the pumps and pipeline infrastructure in working order. No recent demand for drawdowns though, so the work is intermittent. It's really hard on me and my family."

Petrov appeared to be very empathetic to Boudreaux's plight, which he vowed that he shared. On the face of it he was a fellow oil worker of Belarusan extraction. He had a wife and two children. He said that he was a second generation American. But he really was a Russian intelligence officer, living in deep cover as a normal US citizen. He had been extensively trained in US culture, customs, language and accents by the FSB in Russia before being sent to the US, *tabula rasa,* to establish a new identity. He and his family had been given made-up backstories, referred to as their "legends". Over the years they had blended seamlessly into the local community. But behind the veneer of normalcy he, and others like him, were regularly involved in clandestine activities. He would relay messages to his handlers in Moscow by encrypted shortwave radio or hide secret ones in metadata on otherwise innocent images he posted on the internet. But one of his chief duties was the recruitment of American dissidents to the growing secret cell he commanded in his region, of which both the FBI and CIA were well aware. Thus Petrov was extremely interested in fostering a relationship with Boudreaux.

IV

Friday, March 22nd, FBI Headquarters, Washington DC, 09:00 EDT

Special Agent Brian Bretton, Head of the FBI's Anti-Terrorism Unit, was no stranger to the ongoing saga of Albert Stern and the Viking sands. Tall, solid and well ripped, the 45 year old had seen a lot in his FBI career. His square jaw and uncomplicated visage belied his interior strength and resolve. He had worked with the CIA's Chris Wytham from the very beginning as they both tried to apprehend Albert Stern.

Based on reports of heightened internet chatter amongst known domestic terrorists, he had been ordered to assemble his staff to consider appropriate security measures. The chatter seemed to be most threatening towards the US petroleum sector, but it was frustratingly non-specific.

"Sam," he asked his lead agent, "fill us in on what you have been hearing."

"The chatter has been increasing, focused on some kind of preemptive strike against our national energy security infrastructure, Brian. It sounds to our NSA listeners like it's at Russia's instigation, given the recent oil catastrophes in Africa and just now in Saudi Arabia. They totally disavow any complicity in them, of course, nor can our intelligence agencies find any direct attribution or links. But known Russian-financed sleeper cells here seem to be very active participants in the current chatter. Their method of encryption also indicates Russian involvement, although the NSA has been able to break through it."

"What would be a logical target then?" Bretton asked his group of agents.

"Not our very profitable shale oil industry, I wouldn't think." a deputy agent ventured. "It's big, but very diffuse. There are too many small operators. It uses totally unconventional technology. A successful strike against it would be extremely hard."

"Nor against our transcontinental web of transit pipelines." another special agent added. "They are too tightly controlled and monitored. There's often considerable ullage in many of them from time-to-time. Without a master schedule of shipments it would be totally random to hit any one of them. Nor would it disable the system, vast and complex as it is."

"No, you are both right", Bretton concluded. What they seem to target is very large deposits or storage facilities for crude oil."

"Like our SRP?" lead agent Sam ventured. "It's the biggest oil 'deposit' in the US, all neatly contained in a small, interconnected region on the Gulf coast."

"Good thinking, Sam." Bretton acknowledged. "That's what we should move quickly to protect. I'll discuss it immediately with FBI Director Morse. I would expect that he will want me to take a team down to our New Orleans Field Office to coordinate and oversee our surveillance efforts."

V

Monday, March 25th, Zeringue Park near Elmwood, Louisiana, 22:30 CDT

This lightly wooded park remained open until 23:00. On a clear, moonless night Lev Petrov was alone in the dark walking his Russian Borzoi dog. But he was keenly surveying his surroundings, looking for an area of pavement that was full of children's chalk drawings. Near a bench under a large, spreading live oak he finally spotted them.

"From the curved tail of a pink chalk drawing of a cat," he remembered, "take twenty paces to the north, and look for a nearby rubbish bin on a 1.5 meter post. Ah, there it is." A seemingly childish, random pink chalk scribble on the post confirmed that it was the one he was looking for. Just half an hour earlier another man walking his dog had stopped there seemingly to discard some rubbish and clandestinely to mark the pillar with the telltale squiggle of pink chalk. A classic "dead drop". The man was an undercover FSB agent who had been flown in from the Consulate General of the Russian Federation in Houston to deliver a tiny but important parcel from Moscow for Petrov.

Petrov led his dog over to sniff the post while he quickly attended to his own business. He took a Snickers bar out of his pocket and woofed it down. With trained sleight-of-hand he discarded the wrapper and deftly probed between the canister and its plastic garbage bag insert to extract the tiny parcel. He put it into his pocket. Satisfied that no one had seen him, he added a red chalk tick to the post and hurried to leave the park before closing time. Mission accomplished? Perhaps....

VI

Tuesday, March 26th, FBI Field Office, New Orleans, Louisiana, 09:00 CDT

"How has the surveillance gone on Petrov?" Bretton asked his assembled team.

"24/7, sir. It's been very successful. Last night we followed him to a local park in Elmwood where he picked something up from a dead drop. It had been left there earlier by a known FSB undercover agent from Houston. Petrov never saw us and we did nothing to apprehend him, as you had instructed us." an agent replied.

"Perfect. Whatever it was we need to follow him and it to its intended recipient. Something dangerous is clearly afoot."

"What do you think it was, sir?"

"My bet is that it is part of the last quantity on Earth of the devastating weapon that the Russians had secured from Stern. It all but confirms our suspicions that they intend to use it against our SRP. But how and by whom is what we urgently need to know."

"We have agents carefully watching Petrov's sleeper cell, sir. They meet in a bar down by the docks. We noticed that Petrov has been especially friendly lately towards a casual maintenance laborer at the SRP. His name is Armand Boudreaux. We have reason to believe that he has been radicalized and is desperate to earn money to support his family. It certainly looks like his recruitment is underway."

"Put Boudreaux under full surveillance immediately and monitor his contacts with Petrov and other of his cell members. This could be a critical breakthrough." Bretton ordered.

VII

Thursday, March 28th, The Olde Alehouse, Elmwood, Louisiana, 20:30 CDT

Boudreaux entered the back room of the bar and was promptly handed a cold Abita craft beer by Petrov.

"*Merci, mon ami.*" Boudreaux graciously responded. "I really needed that! It was a very hard week."

"*Pas de quoi.*" Petrov replied. "Let's go sit over there in the corner. I have something important to discuss with you."

Away from the rest of the boisterous group, Petrov began his carefully planned hard sell to Boudreaux. "We petroleum workers are purposely undervalued, don't you agree?" he began. "They treat us like disposable pieces of rubbish. It's deplorable. High time for us to make a statement!"

"I agree, but what can we really do to make any significant change in our plight?" Boudreaux answered.

"We must adhere to our socialist values and create a crisis for them before they will ever notice us."

"That would be very hard."

"Not really. Let me explain. It could help us all and be especially lucrative for you and your family."

"Oh, then, please tell me more." Boudreaux said, with growing interest. Petrov was very pleased to see how easily the bait had been taken!

VIII

Monday, April 1st, SRP Texoma Pumping Station, Big Hill, Sabine Parish, Louisiana, 07:00 CDT

Armand Boudreaux arrived early in the morning at the pumping station to help carry out an infrequent SRP inter-deposit transfer. The exercise was merely to keep the critical infrastructure in top operating condition. Nothing new would be added to the reserve, but large quantities of crude would be exchanged via pipeline amongst its four vast, underground storage sites. Boudreaux was grateful for the occasional opportunity to earn some sustenance for his beleaguered family.

But this wouldn't be a normal operation for him. Something unusual had been added to the exercise. Tucked away in his overalls pocket Boudreaux carried a small vial of red sand that had been given to him by Petrov. He didn't really understand what effects it might produce when introduced into the pipeline system, but for the $50,000 he had been promised to deploy it, he didn't really care. "After all, what can such a small amount of red sand possibly do? Probably nothing at all." he mused. In any event, he would follow his instructions in such a way as not to be detected and then collect easy money while others took either the responsibility or the blame.

But Boudreaux never suspected that out of sight and at the ready was an FBI SWAT team led by Bretton. It was carefully observing him.

"Be ready to act the minute he goes to work opening the valves to begin the crude transfer. If you see him go to his pocket, target him for a central body mass shot. I'd like to take him alive, but if he tries to put anything into the open system, shoot to kill. He must be stopped at all costs." Bretton ordered.

Boudreaux was obviously nervous but resolute in carrying out his task. It all seemed so easy and inconsequential. He tried to follow a set routine while not attracting any undue attention. Valves opened and set to commence inter-deposit transfer, he removed a kerchief from his pocket in which he had wrapped the small vial of Viking sands. He opened it furtively and looked carefully at it. That triggered immediate action from the SWAT team.

Charging out from behind a complex of pipes, Bretton yelled "Drop it slowly and fall to the ground, face down! We have you completely surrounded." as Boudreaux could readily see. But, stubbornly, he still wanted to strike a blow for social justice. As he dropped to his knees he reached up to try to dump the sands into the open valve flange of the pipeline. Shots rang out immediately. One was lethal, the others errant. The precious vial of sands was shattered and the small quantity of them that it contained was blown away by the fickle bayou winds. For a second and most critical time the Russians had failed to best their greatest adversary.

PART 7
THE MIDDLE KINGDOM

"Beware the darkness of dragons; beware their talons of power and fire. The hunger of a dragon is slow to wake, but hard to sate."

I

Monday April 8th, Meeting of the PSC, Beijing, PR China, 10:00 GMT +7

The Communist Party's General Secretary had called an emergency meeting of the country's most senior decision-making body, the 7 member Politburo Standing Committee (PSC). While the PSC's collective leadership appeared to make all the important decisions for the government, real and final power had become *de facto* vested in the General Secretary, as his cult of personality continued to grow. Today there was one critical issue to discuss, resolve and fashion into a plan of immediate action.

The Communist Party's grip on China had become more tenuous than it ever had been. The aftermath of the nuclear exchange between Israel and Iran had hit Asia hard. Radioactive fallout had blanketed most of the southern half of the country, coming like a death cloud on the prevailing westerly winds. Many were sick or had already died from radiation poisoning. There had been massive crop failures in the valleys of the Yangtze, Yellow and Mekong Rivers - the breadbaskets and rice bowls of China. Civil unrest was at its highest ever level, as many were forced to riot and loot for their very survival. The People's Liberation Army (PLA) had been mobilized to enforce strict martial law in the major cities, but, countrywide, many soldiers had already deserted to return to their suffering families. Although a fair portion of China's electricity came from coal-fired power plants, the Russian squeeze on crude oil availability was playing havoc with the otherwise energy-hungry but faltering economy of the once booming Middle Kingdom. Indeed, civil society in China was on the very brink of complete chaos when the General Secretary convened his emergency meeting. Something dire and drastic had to be done immediately to ensure the very survival of the Party.

"*Tóngshì*", the General Secretary started, "we must deal decisively and soon with the great menacing bear to our north that has us in a death hug. We have been their traditional allies for many years but there is no longer any reciprocity between us. We must act quickly to secure adequate energy resources for us or we will perish! *Tóngshì* Energy Minister Chen, tell us first what are the Russian oil and gas reserves in nearby Sakhalin, to our northeast?"

"*Dāngrán*, General Secretary. They are estimated to be 15 billion barrels of oil and 2.6 trillion cubic meters of natural gas. We have bought some of this production, but most of it is exported directly to Japan. The areas of Sakhalin now under license account for only 10% of the abundant hydrocarbon reserves of its continental shelf. The existing projects have created infrastructure that can be used by other offshore Sakhalin oil and gas projects in the future. There would be plenty of potential for additional discoveries and production in the hands of a new overlord State."

"Exactly. And what are our own estimated reserves in the far west Tarim Basin?"

"It is still substantially underexplored, although we have at least 500 million proved reserves there already."

"So we must protect our northwestern flank from the Russians while plundering Sakhalin." the General Secretary concluded. "They have given us no other choice, colleagues."

"But Sakhalin 1 is operated by ExxonMobil." Chen rejoined. "That would put us in direct conflict with both the Russians and the Americans."

"Indeed, that's true, *Tóngshì* Chen, but I would wager that the Americans would have no stomach for direct involvement in a conflict once again in Asia, especially not to protect Russian interests, even if it is at a price to one of their own. Besides, the naive businessman American President knows nothing of either natural resources or diplomacy. We have already seen that he can be easily manipulated and intimidated. I charge you all to deliver to me a detailed action plan for the invasion and occupation of Sakhalin in no more than a fortnight. We cannot wait any longer or we will lose our grip on our country! Meeting adjourned."

II

The petroleum reserves of the Sakhalin Producing Complex coveted by the Chinese were composed of four producing fields - Chayvo, Odoptu, Piltun-Astokhskoye (Sakhalin 2) and the Arkutun-Dagi field (Sakhalin 1). The latter is operated by a wholly owned subsidiary of American oil giant, ExxonMobil, co-venturing with Japan's SODECO. The fields are located off the northeast coast of Sakhalin Island in the Sea of Okhotsk. Total daily production from the Complex exceeded 300,000 bbls/day.

Production from Sakhalin 1 field is routed through the existing Chayvo onshore processing facility on Sakhalin Island and delivered through pipelines to the De-Kastri oil export terminal located in Khabarovsk Krai, on the Russian mainland.

In addition, Sakhalin 2 had also been in production for over a decade. The project is led by the Sakhalin Energy Investment Company, which is a joint venture between Russia's Gazprom (50% plus 1 "golden share") and minority partners Royal Dutch/Shell Group and subsidiaries of Japan's Mitsui and Mitsubishi Corporations.

In the Sakhalin region, temperatures can drop to -45 degrees Celsius (-49° Fahrenheit) in winter. Arctic winds combine with high humidity for a wind-chill factor of -70°C (-94°F). At such temperatures, people can work outside on land and at sea only in short shifts, despite steel cladding on the outer sides of the offshore platforms that break the wind and offer them some scant protection. The sea around the Sakhalin Production Complex is covered in ice for six months of the year and therefore production is limited to the ice-free late spring and summer months.

III

Tuesday, April 16th, Central Military Commission HQ, Beijing, PR China, 10:00 GMT +7

Lieutenant General Zhao Xin had just received his Top-Secret orders to implement Operation *Liè Xióng* (Bear Hunt). All units of the Shenyang Military District in the Northern Theater Command of the PLA were to be mobilized immediately for imminent foreign action. Their objectives would be fourfold: to take the oil export base to Japan at the port of Prigorodnoye, on the southern tip of Sakhalin island, where the Shell feeder pipelines from the offshore oil fields converged; to secure the crude oil marine export terminal at De-Kastri in northern Sakhalin, where the main Exxon pipeline crossed the Tatar Strait and continued on to Khabarovsk and Vladivostok on the Russian mainland; to subdue and occupy Yuzhno-Sakhalinsk, the island's administrative center and largest city; and, as the most immediate and critical of these objectives, simultaneously to seize the four offshore oil producing fields and cut off their oil flow through the pipelines to Siberian Russia.

It would appear that the PSC in Beijing had been reading and re-reading the timeless advice of ancient military strategist, Sun Tzu. He had counseled that, *"In war, the way is to avoid what is strong and strike at what is weak…the whole secret lies in confusing the enemy so that he cannot fathom our real intent."* So prior to launching a strike on Sakhalin, China would have to fake a belligerent diversion elsewhere, as far west as possible from Sakhalin and from their contentious Amur River border with Russia, where such a pre-emptive strike would have been most expected. The isolated Kuzuyak Pass, threading through the towering Altai mountains from the extreme northwest of China's Xinjiang Province to the cities and oil basins of Russian southwestern Siberia, would be the place instead.

IV

Monday, April 22nd, Field Operations, PLA Western Theater Command, Kuzuyak Pass, PR China, 08:00 GMT +7

"Hand me the field glasses." General Chen Yu, Commandant of the PLA's Western Theater Command, ordered his adjutant. Thoughtfully he put them up to his eyes to survey his troops' movements through the Kuzuyak Pass. All appeared to be proceeding so far as planned with Operation *Dōngfēng* (East Wind).

"We don't seem to have been detected yet by the Russians, General, but shouldn't we have been doing this at night, heavily camouflaged?" his adjutant asked.

"That's not what my orders were. We want them to see us massing on their unmanned border."

From the high ground at the top of the pass the theater of action opened below them onto the vast West Siberian Plain, looking north towards some of Russia's most prolific oil fields in the Western Siberia Basin. The closest airfields and military bases of the Russian Red Army were within range of artillery fire from the PLA's heavily fortified positions atop the pass.

"Are we ready to advance, General?" the adjunct continued. "Shall I pass that on as your orders, sir?"

"No, of course not! Order all units to dig in and wait instead, with our artillery and tanks prominently visible to any opposition who materialize below. We will be protected by air cover, but only if we need it."

"Yes, sir, but we will be completely exposed to their land and air forces." the adjutant replied with a worried look.

"We hold the high ground. We are still 100 meters from the border, but we haven't fired a shot yet. We will not advance any further. Let them puzzle over our motives while we fulfill our orders. Just as Sun Tzu counseled us, *"Let your plans be dark and impenetrable as night... He will win who knows when to fight and when not to fight. It is more important to out think your enemy than to out fight him."*

And so the great subterfuge had successfully begun.

V

Tuesday, April 23rd, General Staff Building, HQ of the Russian Armed Forces, Moscow, 07:00 GMT +3

A weary General Konstantin Volkov looked with great alarm at the continuous stream of field dispatches and aerial reconnaissance data that had been rapidly coming in from Red Army military outposts in South Central Siberia. A stocky, somewhat disheveled old veteran in his early 70s, he had both been through and seen everything in war. But he simply couldn't believe what he was seeing now. Neither could FSB Chief, Chestnoy, who had hurried over from his office in the Lubyanka to confer personally with Volkov. These two old comrades-in-arms were also good friends. They had come up together through the ranks in parallel to the President's rise to his own political apex.

"We suddenly have massive PLA troop movements along our southern border with China, *Vanya*. Where does your intel tell us that they are headed and why? What could this all possibly mean?" Volkov asked.

"We're as puzzled as you, *Kostya*, but there could be at least one very dire explanation."

"Tell me, *Vanya*, what would that be?"

"We both know well that ever since the Iranian-Israeli nuclear exchange the world has been reeling from critical oil shortages and unheard of prices. The Chinese must be suffering very badly, especially since they have no significant oil resources of their own. Perhaps they are after some of ours? It would be a reckless gambit, but these are desperate times."

"I hadn't fully considered that possibility, *Vanya*." Volkov replied. "Assuming that you are right, though, would they dare challenge us so boldly? Do they really think that they could take our oilfields in Western Siberia? That's over 81 billion well-guarded barrels."

"Their Belt and Road initiative includes a Trans-Altai pipeline to feed their hungry oil market. It was to be a joint venture with us, but maybe they plan to build it themselves?"

"Anyway, *Vanya*, I have informed the President and I am awaiting his guidance. Clearly we need to stop the perfidious Chinese in their tracks."

"But don't you find it curious, *Kostya*, that they've stopped just short of our border, bristling with armaments, but without a shot having yet been fired by them?"

"Indeed, but we still need to pin them down where they are. I am ordering all units of our Joint Strategic Command Central to mobilize their armored units and infantry and to move forward to confront the aggressors immediately. I've also requested full air and armed drone coverage to blanket the theater of operations completely. The Chinese will not dare to cross our border in the face of such formidable opposition."

"Yes, *Kostya*, but remember that their technology and weaponry is as good as ours and their land forces vastly outnumber us. There could be immense slaughter!"

"Be that as it may, *Vanya*, I am sure that our Commander in Chief will order us to finish what the Chinese have foolishly started."

The die was irrevocably cast. The great Chinese hoax was succeeding masterfully.

VI

Friday, April 26th, Port *of* Prigorodnoye, southern tip of Sakhalin Island, Russia, 09:00 GMT +11

Through the early morning mist cloaking the harbor Port Superintendent, Genadi Pacenko, could just begin to make out the shadowy outlines of several very large vessels on the horizon. He assumed them to be the heavily laden transport ships that were scheduled to dock soon at the offloading facilities of the port. Their arrival with consumer goods and farming equipment would stoke the normal excitement amongst the residents of nearby Yuzhno-Sakhalinsk, the island's administrative center and largest city, where its 171,000 souls struggled to eke out a hard scrabble fishing and agrarian living. Many of the men were 'roughneck' and 'roustabout' casual laborers in the petroleum industry as well.

In this harsh region temperatures can drop to well below 0 Celsius in winter. Arctic winds can sometimes combine with high humidity to produce a wind-chill factor of greater than -70°C. At such temperatures, people can work outside only for very short periods. The sea around Sakhalin is covered in ice for six months of the year and therefore most outdoor work is limited to only the ice-free months.

"Have we had radio confirmation from the ships yet of their proposed landing schedules?" Pacenko asked his radio operator.

"*Da, Nachalnik*, they are requesting pilots to guide them through the channel and tugs to bring them in."

"Everything is normal then. Dispatch the pilots and 4 tugs."

Satisfied, Pacenko continued to scan the horizon for both developing weather patterns and for any other vessels in the shipping lanes that could inadvertently interfere with the safe docking of such behemoth ships. On the far horizon he thought he saw several smaller ships moored, but he couldn't be sure due to the fog and mist rising from the roiling sea. "Probably factory fishing boats from northern Japan." he thought, but their configuration didn't seem exactly to fit that mold. Indeed, they looked more like military vessels, but there was no reason to believe that they were. Some tensions over ownership of the string of Kuril Islands between Sakhalin and Hokkaido still existed with Japan, but there hadn't been any hostilities over them for many years.

In due course the first 800 foot ship in the flotilla of cargo transporters was guided in and moored alongside the offloading pier. The *Serene Dragon*, convenience-flagged out of Aruba, was a roll-on/roll-off vessel designed and equipped to allow up to 500 civilian, commercial or military vehicles to be easily loaded and then driven off. A huge clang resounded throughout the harbor from the impact of the ship's heavy metal ramp slamming down on the pier in preparation for it to begin offloading its cargo.

Pacenko scanned the pre-cleared manifest on his tablet. "This should be the first part of the shipment. Dongfeng farm tractors and tillers from Wuhan." he thought to himself. "The LandWind X7 knock offs of Land Rover's Defender SUV must be on the *Emperor Kangxi*, next in the queue." But he was both surprised and dismayed to see that the latter ship was already maneuvering into position at the two-berth pier to unload simultaneously. "That's not supposed to happen!" he complained vehemently to the radio operator.

It was too late. The *Emperor Kangxi's* huge offloading ramp slammed down onto the pier next to that of the *Serene Wind's* and throaty roars of engines starting up reverberated from within the bowels of both mammoth ships.

"What the hell! We can't handle simultaneous offloading!" a perplexed Pacenko this time stammered to his radio operator. "Hail the captain of the *Emperor Kangxi* and tell him to cease and desist until the *Serene Wind's* vehicles are offloaded and driven to our holding lots."

Too late again. Totally ignoring Pacenko's orders, vehicles started emerging from both ships. But they certainly weren't what he had expected! No tractors, tillers and SUVs. Rather, camouflage-painted dull olive and tan ZTZ-99A2 main battle tanks bearing the Chinese red star and armed with long-range 125mm 50-caliber ZPT98 smoothbore cannons capable of firing deadly APFSDS rounds of depleted uranium. Some pointed their cannons directly at Pacenko's shabby HQ shack. Others took aim at strategic locations in the sleepy city beyond. Following the convoy of tanks were both WZ-551B armored personnel carriers and diesel trucks brimming over with heavily armed squadrons of elite Chinese Marines. The total picture was a package of overwhelming force, more than sufficient to take and hold the port of Prigorodnoye.

Panicked, frightened and overwhelmed, Pacenko snapped some hasty pictures of the incredible scene with his iPhone to send on to the HQ of the Russian high military command. He was completely unprotected, as the small garrison of Russian port guards had fled in haste the minute they saw the hopeless situation developing.

As if all of that wasn't enough, the next thing Pacencko saw completely unnerved him. Flying very low from over the eastern horizon was a squadron of twin-engine, medium-weight FC-31 stealth fighters originating from the latest model Chinese aircraft carrier, the *Chengdu*, anchored well out of sight over the horizon. The jets menacingly circled the port and then proceeded north to give air cover to the rumbling convoy which, having easily taken the Port of Prigorodnoye without firing a shot, was headed further on to capture both the crude oil marine export terminal at De-Kastri in northern Sakhalin and Yuzhno-Sakhalinsk, the island's administrative center.

The closer vessels just on the horizon that Pacenko had assumed were Japanese commercial fishing factory ships were actually a cluster of Type 075 Chinese amphibious assault ships, able to carry an estimated 30 helicopters and hundreds of troops. From them waves of Z-10 attack helicopters and Z-18 troop transport choppers skirted the eastern shore of the island and headed directly for the string of production platforms on Sakhalin's northeast corner. Their mission would be to both take and secure the string of offshore oilfields that produced the 15 billion barrels of crude oil and associated natural gas that the Chinese so desperately needed.

Circling high above all of this chaos, like an all-seeing eye, was a JD-600, the newest Chinese AWACS plane, with a detection range of several hundred kilometers. Assisted by a satellite link, it was busy detecting and jamming the navigation and controls of the late arriving Russian fighter planes. The PLA thus held complete domination over both the land and sea in the entire theater of operations. Inexorably, the long column of Chinese armor and troops moved steadily to take its objectives and to secure its resource prizes.

VII

Friday, April 26th, General Staff Building, HQ of the Russian Armed Forces, Moscow, 08:00 GMT +3

Already having resolved to stop the Chinese dead in their tracks at the Kuzuyak Pass, General Volkov was totally shocked to read the latest coded dispatches flooding in detailing the Chinese surprise attack on Sakhalin. He quickly realized that they had fallen prey to an elaborate Chinese ruse. The majority of his troops were now committed to the standoff at Russia's southern border with China, leaving scant few to stop the rapid Chinese advance on Sakhalin Island. The Red Army's Joint Strategic Command East that oversees and protects the normally peaceful territories of Sakhalin and Kamchatka was severely depleted. Recent massive transfers of men and munitions from that theater had been made to the west to assist the Red Army's Western Command in its attempted occupation of the newly "independent" Donetsk and Luhansk Republics in the Donbas region, in the process of being seized from Ukraine. The distance from the Kuzuyak pass to Sakhalin was greater than 6,000 kilometers over rugged, barren and often impassable terrain. The logistics of moving troops and armor rapidly east was a nightmare. And it would probably be much too late anyway.

"*Bozhe moi*, we're faced with a *fait accompli!*" Volkov groaned to his adjunct, Colonel Vladimir Kalashnik.

"Yes, sir, we certainly didn't anticipate this."

"But we must do what we can to stop them immediately. What news is coming in from our 11th and 12th Air Defense Forces in Khabarovsk and Vladivostok? Surely our MiG-31K's and Su-24 series fighters can blunt the tip of the advancing Chinese spear?"

"Nothing good, sir. We scrambled them all but they were 500 km away. Then the Chinese electronic jamming capabilities rendered their navigation and control systems ineffective. Rockets and missiles have missed their mark consistently and several of our aircraft have crashed out of control. There doesn't seem to be anything we can do to stop them. They were too well prepared."

"*Yebena mat'!*" Volkov exclaimed anxiously. "How will I ever explain this to the President?"

VIII

Monday, April 29th, The President's Executive Office, the Kremlin, Moscow, Russia, 09:00 GMT +3

Generals Volkov and Chestnoy had been rapidly summoned to the Kremlin for a private meeting with the President. They both had dreaded but expected it.

"*Zdravstvuyte, Gospodin President.*" Volkov began timidly upon entering the President's office. But as usual, the President wanted to get straight down to the matters at hand. He commenced to give them both a withering dressing down.

"This is an unspeakable humiliation for us!" the President raged. He continued with unrelenting invective for over five minutes while both Volkov and Chestnoy cowered and slumped in their chairs. What could they possibly say?

"We are working on a new plan to stop the Chinese advance,

sir." Chestnoy tried to interject.

"I already have one." the President icily replied. "With time and patience, we can turn this unthinkable debacle into a full victory for us. We will let the Chinese silkworms munch on the sweet mulberry leaves of their temporary conquest while they grow fat in their complacency. Once they are sleeping in their supposedly secure cocoons, we will strike them swiftly and decisively. Keep up the highest level of surveillance on their actions. When I give the order, we will take a page out of our old friend Saddam's playbook, when he was forced to abandon Kuwait. We will launch a counterattack on our traitorous former allies when they least expect it."

"I'm sure it will be a very clever stratagem." Volkov ventured. For the first time in a week both he and Chestnoy was feeling a bit less tense. But only momentarily. In his ever-vindictive manner, the President had one last bombshell to drop on the two of them.

"One final matter to deal with, *tovarishchi.*" the President continued. "The time is quickly coming for you both to retire. You have served the Motherland and me long and mostly well. But I believe that it is time to interject new blood. You two old Cold Warriors will never get up to speed on current developments in information technology, weaponry, cyber warfare and espionage as such things exist in today's *realpolitik*. So you both will oversee this last retaliatory operation against the Chinese; tutor and train your successors; and then gracefully fade away. I will make it worth it for both of you, commensurate with your long service. Dismissed."

THE VIKING SANDS : ENDGAME

IX

Sunday, May 12th, Sakhalin Producing Complex, Sea of Okhotsk, offshore Sakhalin Island, Russia, 06:00 GMT +11

All was quiet on the numerous producing platforms and satellite structures that comprised the chain of the Sakhalin Production Complex, lying some 15 kilometers offshore in the stormy Sea of Okhotsk. Only skeletal crews of newly trained Chinese oil workers were on duty over the weekend. The morning sun was just rising in the east, spreading its rosy fingers over the far horizon. It was reasonable for these few maintenance workers on duty at the various sites to expect it to be just another quiet and uneventful day of a long, boring weekend. That was exactly what the Russians were counting on.

Only 50 kilometers away to the northeast and closing fast, a lethal storm was coming. Flying low over the waves to avoid radar detection, squadrons of fifth generation Russian Su-57 fighter bombers and MIG-31K Foxhound escorts, were launched in sorties from the *Chengdu*. Bristling with sophisticated, laser-guided rockets and smart bombs, they were headed straight for the platforms of the Sakhalin Complex and for the ULCC tankers moored at them. Each such tanker was already loaded with the first 2.2 million barrel shipments of crude oil to be transported via the Yellow Sea to China's mammoth Qingdao crude oil-receiving port in Shandong Province. Recent improvements to the Russians' electronic countermeasures would assure that any Chinese jamming attempts would not deter them this time. Coming out of the sun behind them, they would be almost impossible to see until they were well over their targets.

Back at the Russian General Staff HQ in Moscow, both Volkov and Chestnoy were sitting before a giant LED screen watching the incoming satellite feed of the retaliatory plan that the President had ordered to be put into action. They were both soon joined by Lieutenant General Vasili Sokolov, Commander-in-Chief of the Russian Air Force. Mercilessly and with overwhelming force, the Russian air armada, like a swarm of angry hornets, targeted the many wellheads on each of the platforms and obliterated them with potent incendiary ordinance. Huge explosions rocked the platforms and massive fireballs of crude oil and natural gas burning out of control lit the morning sky up into a hellish inferno. All of the ULCCs were slammed with supersonic KH-41 "Sunburn" anti-ship missiles, sinking them in seas of flames. In minutes the devastation was utter and complete. All production capabilities were totally destroyed. The Chinese may have seized control of the Sakhalin distribution infrastructure, but it would now be useless to them without access to the critical oil resources that they had tried to steal.

"Have we made this seeming sacrifice of 300,000 barrels a day of our production needlessly, though?" Sokolov wondered out loud.

" No, *Vásja*, we haven't really lost anything." Chestnoy replied. "None of the oil from the Sakhakin Complex was being used for our internal consumption nor was it being profitably sold for export. Instead it was all committed to the Japanese under concessionary, evergreen supply contracts, negotiated under Gorbachev's fanciful *glasnost* initiatives. We were barely even earning back our production costs. Unwittingly, the Chinese struck at their Japanese neighbor's vital economic interests, not at ours. Now they will have to deal with Tokyo's wrath while we are completely vindicated for simply protecting our own national interests."

X

Quickly the Chinese licked their wounds and began an orderly withdrawal from their failed, high-risk gambit on Sakhalin. The Russians unceasingly dogged them from overhead. They could have mercilessly harassed and slaughtered them from the air - as did the US-led Coalition when the Iraqis withdrew from Kuwait - but the President chose instead to leave them to their ignominious retreat, thinking, perhaps, that they could possibly be of future use to him in his ongoing battle with NATO over the status of the Ukraine. Discretion being the better part of valor, he realized that Chinese would always be a powerful neighbor with whom Russia must deal.

In just under a month's time both Chestnoy and Volkov had retired to their newly gifted *dachas* after due pomp and ceremony. Newly promoted Lieutenant Generals Lukhzov and Kalashnik had taken their places. The torch had been successfully passed to the next generation of Russian spies and warriors.

PART 8
REDEMPTION AND REVENGE

"A good act does not nullify a bad one, nor a bad act a good one. Each should have its own particular consequences."

I

Wednesday, May 1st, Director of Intelligence Baker's Office, Headquarters, Langley, Virginia, 10:00 EDT

What then to do with Albert Stern? Clearly he could be put away in solitary confinement for the rest of his life in the brutal, super-max federal security prison in Florence, Colorado. Or he could have an indefinite stay in the military detention facility at Guantanamo Bay. But he couldn't be executed, as the administration in Washington years ago had issued an Executive Order permanently abolishing the death penalty for all federal prisoners. It was a vexing puzzle; but, perhaps, it also presented a unique opportunity?

"Stern has recovered his memory and we have completely debriefed him." Wytham told the Director and the assembled group of agents and analysts. He is repentant, but still confused and ashamed. It would be quite easy to turn him into an expendable asset, if we so chose."

"How and why so?" Director Baker asked.

"We still need his help, Tim. He revealed to us that there is still a small cache of the Viking sands hidden at his *estancia* in Patagonia. We need to retrieve it immediately. Otherwise we have none and the Russians might still have just enough to do catastrophic damage to us. We don't know the amount that they used of the vial Stern surrendered to them to take out the Saudis nor whether the amount lost in their attempt on our SPR was the final end of their supply."

"But the Russians have their hands full right now with both the Chinese and the Ukrainians, Chris. I doubt that another strike against us is high on their agenda."

"Still, it's inevitable in the long run, Tim. It would complete the last piece of their master plan to achieve world economic domination. It's only a matter of time."

"And so what do you recommend for us to do now, Chris?"

"Clearly we need to consider making a preemptive strike against their vast petroleum resources before they move again to destroy our own. And that's where Stern can help us."

"Really? How so?"

"Well, it's clear that he knows better than anyone else how to deploy the weapon most effectively. Nor has he ever been hesitant to do so. His track record of reckless ruin worldwide without remorse demonstrates that conclusively."

"First he has to lead us to the last cache of the sands, though." Baker observed.

"Yes, but we may have another option as well."

"Like what, Chris?"

"Well, we observed the entire fiery descent and crash of the *TLK* spacecraft on the Kazakh steppes with high resolution surveillance cameras from our orbiting satellites. We kept watch on the wreckage to see if the Russians or the Kazakhs sent a recovery party. But before either could we saw some Kazakh nomads combing through the scattered debris. They recovered some kind of canister, apparently still intact, and hastily left with it. My bet is that it is full of Martian soil. If so, we stymied the brazen mission but failed to destroy its sole purpose. Somewhere out there could be enough of the sands to wreak untold further havoc if they fall into the wrong hands. While it's still crucial to recover the tiny cache in Patagonia, it's even more critical to track the nomads and to relieve them of such a dangerous weapon."

"Do we still have them under close surveillance, Chris?"

"We did until they reached Almaty. It's very unusual for nomads to go into such an urban setting. Clearly they are looking to sell the canister, most probably knowing nothing of its lethal contents. It's a nightmare scenario. They were last seen entering the huge, tented central bazaar, where we lost eyes on them."

"Who do we have on the ground there, Chris?"

"Dick Brooks is Chief of Station at our embassy in the capital, Nur-Sultan. He had been posted earlier in Buenos Aires when we tried to apprehend Stern there. He knows all about the lethal Viking sands. I will call him immediately and have him put agents into the field urgently to track down the nomads. I only hope they haven't sold the canister to anyone yet!"

"Fine, Chris. Let's get moving fast. This is much too dangerous a situation already. It must have top priority. We will just have to consider what ultimately to do with Stern at another time."

"Leave that with me, Tim. I have some interesting ideas worth exploring. But we will need some clandestine help from our biggest major, Global Oil, to pull it off. I will have a talk with Secretary Finlay at the DOE to see what we can arrange with them. He and Global's Chairman, Kelly, go back together a long way."

"OK. Report back to me on it daily." Baker ordered.

II

Friday, May 3rd, Zelenyy Bazaar, Almaty, Kazakhstan, 08:00 GMT +6

Nomads Kasym and Ablai were very uneasy in an urban setting. But they had business to do as they entered the vast bazaar. Mostly a green market, it nevertheless had a section where traders in durable goods and antiquities had their offices and stalls. They were looking for one particular wily trader with whom they had done occasional business before.

Tumar Lermontov was of mixed Russian/Kazahk descent. He had fashioned a very profitable import/export business dealing mostly illegally in antiquities and objects of cultural interest. He always looked forward to what nomads would occasionally bring to him from their chance finds on the steppes.

"*Salem*, Tumar!" Kasym greeted the proprietor, sharing with him a firm handshake.

"*Salamatsyn ba*, old friend. What have you brought for me this time?"

Ablai greeted Tumar as well and then slung the camel saddlebag off his shoulder. Reaching in he withdrew the scorched canister and placed it on a tray table in front of Lermantov.

"What is this piece of junk?" Lermontov remarked with a clear tone of surprise and disdain.

"Not junk at all. It fell from the sky. It is something very rare and unusual." Ablai ventured. "Surely it has great value!"

"It's probably just a remnant of an obsolete weather satellite that fell from orbit." Lermontov continued. But as he eyed the canister with feigned disinterest, he knew immediately what it really was. He had his ears out in every direction and he was well aware of the story about the Kazakh spacecraft that had crashed to Earth recently on the empty steppes. This was clearly a piece of it! Moreover, he maintained covert contacts that were quite exceptional for a seemingly simple tradesman. The Russian FSB had him on their list of reliable sources.

"Something inside it." he said, as he shook it gently. "Let's see what it is." With this he labored to pry it open. As the sealed top grudgingly gave way he saw a small pile of rich red sand inside. He was stunned, but concealed it well from his two guests. "Just some useless sand." he said. "Not worth anything, really. But since, as you say, it fell from space it might be an interesting curiosity for someone. I can offer you 10,000 Tenge at most for it." Lermontov was anxious to close the deal.

"Disappointing," said Tumar, "but it certainly doesn't contain gold or jewels." he said with a slight smile. "How about 20,000 Tenge to seal the deal?"

Lermontov feigned hesitation but he was quite intent on acquiring the object. "OK, old friends, but next time bring me some interesting ancient artifacts instead."

"Agreed. *Salem*, Tumar!" They all exchanged hearty handshakes.

The two nomads left Lermontov's small shop. Seeing the back of them he simply couldn't believe his luck. The FSB had told him to be on the lookout for nomads trying to sell a piece of space debris. If, indeed, what it was full of was what he had both heard of and read about - the destructive Martian sands - it was an amazing prize! "It will make me rich beyond belief!" he mused. It would just be a question of contacting the FSB, or even ISIS, with whom he also sympathized.

III

Monday, May 6th, El Calafate International Airport, Santa Cruz Province, Patagonia, Argentina 19:00 GMT -3

In the early hours of dusk an unremarkable Gulfstream C-20G aircraft taxied to a halt in front of the small terminal. Out of it three figures emerged, one of which was Albert Stern. Chris Wytham and a fellow agent from the Buenos Aires station led him down the steps, where, at the foot of which, the three of them hastily boarded a waiting black Chevy Tahoe SUV with tinted windows. It pulled quickly out of the parking area and began the uncomfortable, dusty 214 km trip to Stern's *estancia,* just outside of El Chalten.

Just over 3 hours later the SUV pulled in front of the *estancia's* ramshackle, old main residence. Albert was spirited quickly inside.

" Show us where you have hidden the sands." Wytham ordered Stern.

" This way," he replied, "they're in the shearing shed." Albert led them to the dank little outbuilding where the old *gaucho*, Carlos, had been purposely electrocuted a few months earlier. He went to the far corner and asked someone to hand him a shovel. Digging carefully he unearthed a tanned sheep's bladder wrapped in heavy plastic sheeting. From inside it he extracted a small vial of deep red sands that he handed over to Wytham.

"The last of your store?" Wytham asked.

"The very last." Stern replied.

Satisfied, Wytham pocketed the prize and ordered the SUV's driver to take them to the low-key Hosteria Senderos in El Chalten, where they would spend the night. Wytham began to ruminate over the evolving situation. Maybe he had the last few grams of Viking sands left on Earth? But maybe the Russians still had some

THE VIKING SANDS : ENDGAME

left themselves? If so, perhaps through back channels it could be made known to them that such a situation could guarantee mutually assured destruction of each's priceless petroleum resources if either attempted a preemptive strike. An unsatisfactory stalemate, he thought, given the Russians' master plan for world economic domination and their earlier abortive attempt to hit the US's SRP. But for now it would have to do.

What then of the mysterious canister that the nomads had recovered from the wreckage of *TLK*, Wytham wondered? Where was it now and what did it contain? If it was full of Martian soil it would be a whole different ball game, he thought, depending on whom ultimately got their hands on it!

Tuesday, May 7th, Zelenyy Bazaar, Almaty, Kazakhstan, 21:00 GMT +6

Lermantov sat nervously sipping sweet mint tea inside his small office in the bazaar. He was high with anticipation of what his invited bidders would offer him for the canister full of Martian sands. He had reached out to both his contacts in ISIS and in the FSB. The asking price would be at least $1 million.

At the appointed hour a tall, bearded figure in typical *fedayeen* dress appeared at his doorway. He was carrying a heavy saddlebag, presumably stuffed with cash.

"*Salem.*" the ISIS fighter greeted Lermontov. "Let us make a deal." But waiting quietly in the shadows, FSB agents, Borisenko and Fortunatov, were keenly observing the scene. They too had a heavy stash of cash if necessary, but they had no real intention of paying anything. They would let the ISIS fighter strike a deal and then waylay him.

When the fighter opened his saddlebag and dumped $1 million

in neatly bundled $100 bills on the tray before Lermantov, the temptation was far too great. Why bother with the FSB, he thought, when I can already have what I want? He immediately accepted the fighter's generous offer. A handshake sealed the deal. The fighter tucked the scorched canister away into the now empty saddlebag and bid Lermantov a farewell *Salem*. What Lermantov would never know, though, nor could he have detected, was that he had just sold the priceless sands to ISIS for $1million in the finest North Korean-printed counterfeit US currency on the planet.

As the ISIS fighter walked quickly down the dimly lit aisles of the bazaar, the Russians furtively followed him. Had he come alone? Did he have many comrades backing him up? If so, where were they? Where best to seize and throttle him? The answers came quickly.

"*Hal'ant hunak fi alnatq*? Are you there?" the fighter asked softly in Arabic into the shadows.

"*Nem swtyana*, is it done?" came a reply.

"Of course. He will be shocked, though, when he tries to pass on some of the counterfeit cash!"

The Russians paused to count the fighter's support team. There were two tall men with bandolier bullet straps across their chests and AK 47s at the ready standing by a black Mercedes sedan with its engine idling softly. But Borisenko and Fortunatov had the advantages of cover, darkness and surprise. They each screwed silencers on to their FSB OTs-38 service revolvers and targeted their adversaries. "Pop, pop" came dull thuds from each lethal weapon as the two backup men fell dead to the ground before they could return fire. They never knew what hit them. Panicked, the remaining ISIS fighter lunged for safety behind the Mercedes. But two more muted pops dispatched him before he could find adequate cover. Hearing the commotion Lermantov foolishly came out of the bazaar to see what was happening and received a *coup de grace* bullet in the middle of his forehead.

"Put the saddle bag into their car, *Arkasha.*" Borisenko ordered.

"OK, Colonel. Where to?" Fortunatov replied as he took the wheel.

"Back into central Almaty. I'll show you where to park. We will leave for Moscow tomorrow morning."

Fortunatov drove the Mercedes to an appointed spot in a downtown hotel's guest parking lot where the two dumped it. A waiting, unmarked car took them immediately to the Russian consulate with their prize. At 08:00 the next morning a small Russian military transport aircraft took off from Almaty airport with both of them aboard. Looking out the window as the city receded below them, Borisenko remarked how very pleased the President would be.

"Indeed, Colonel. *Atlitchna!*" Fortunatov cheerfully replied.

By the time Chris Wytham and his special-ops group finally reached the entrance to the bazaar, all they found was four men lying dead on the parched, sandy soil with no sign of the scorched canister anywhere.

IV

Wednesday, May 8th, Biological Weapons Facility outside Yekaterinburg, Sverdlovsk Oblast, Urals, Russia, 08:00 GMT +5

When the space canister arrived in Moscow it was flown immediately to a former Soviet biological weapons facility in the country's Urals mountain region. While Russia was a party to the multilateral Biological and Toxins Weapons Convention renouncing the use of such weapons, it was common knowledge that it continued clandestinely to carry out experiments in biological and chemical warfare. The faculty was so top secret that it had no public address nor did it appear on any map. It was the perfect place to hide, secure and test the newly arrived Martian soil.

Evgeni Oblonsky was the lead scientist charged with the sensitive duty of re-verifying the destructive effectiveness of the latest batch of Martian sands. Experiments would be carried out in a sterile lab that was set up according to the strictest rules of health and safety. It was a sealed "clean room", painstakingly assembled with aseptic technology and enclosed in thick, blast proof concrete walls. The only entrance was through a massive, hermetically sealable steel door. All areas were monitored with microscopic "coupon" slides distributed around the perimeters. They were cultured daily to see if any microbiological populations or biochemical contamination had gotten in and what countermeasures had to be taken to deal with them. Chemical cleansing was also performed on all testing surfaces. Everyone was required to wear a sterile over-garment and mask. No chances would be taken that any microbe or biochemical agent could get in to give false readings

"Ready to start our first test?" Oblonsky asked his small team.

"*Da*, sir." his primary assistant, Ilya, responded.

"Set up the test apparatus inside the blast-proof enclosure and get ready to start the fuel drip. We'll quickly see if the sands still have a voracious appetite for light, sweet crude oil." With that a tiny portion of the sands was placed into the test apparatus' sealed chamber and everyone scurried behind the massive door to view the anticipated reaction through its 6" thick, super-hardened glass panel.

As the two substances began to combine in the experiment apparatus anticipation was high. Everyone braced for a burst of searing heat and the sudden appearance of a ghostly blue-white aura as the sands began to commence consuming the crude oil in violent fashion. But as moments passed, enigmatically, nothing seemed to be happening.

This would be a catastrophic failure of the highest order. It just couldn't be, Oblonsky thought. He feared having to report it to anxiously awaiting senior authorities. There had to be a plausible explanation!

"Ilya, bring me the satellite topo maps of the Martian surface immediately!" Oblonsky ordered.

"*Vot*, sir." Ilya replied.

With a knot in the pit of his stomach Oblonsky studied them carefully. He could see the remnants of the American landing site at Chryse Planitia, from where the original sands had come. He also located the site from where *TLK* had taken its sample. The difference struck him immediately. The former was in a soft, cratered, rolling plain latticed with channels and runnels where water had obviously flowed in eons past. But the latter was in the thick, hardened lava "sea", Daedalia Planum, which had been created by vast, ancient volcanic eruptions. It wasn't the chosen landing site but it was where the spacecraft had come down. In the haste and secrecy of the forbidden mission, not enough thought had really been given to optimizing a collection site. "Martian soil is all uniform, right?" Oblonsky thought. But clearly it was not.

No one still knew what was the chemical or biological trigger that produced the voracious reaction to hydrocarbons by the original sands, but it seemed obvious that it was absent from this batch. This was an unmitigated disaster. Billions of rubles wasted and national security recklessly risked just to bring back a batch of unreactive soil? The consequences would be immense!

"*Bozhe moi*, Ilya," Oblonsky groaned, "this is the end for me! Somehow I will be blamed. Perhaps they will only exile me to a menial post in Magnitogorsk, I pray?"

"More likely to the Siberian *gulags*." Ilya replied wryly.

V

Monday, May 13th, Office of the Secretary of Energy, Washington, DC, 11:00 EDT

Energy Secretary Finlay had invited the Chairman of Global Oil Co. to Washington for an off the record chat. Perhaps "invite" wasn't quite the appropriate word. Chairman George Kelly had been summoned from his Plano, Texas, headquarters on an urgent and confidential basis. He was flown to DC on a military transport jet that had landed at a remote area of Andrews AFB, away from the eyes of both the public and the press. A small motorcade was waiting to take him from there, unnoticed, to the DOE.

Global was the US's largest international oil company. Spawned originally from the breakup of the Standard Oil Trust in 1911, it had voraciously devoured many of its brother and sister companies over the years until it reached the top of the heap. It had E&P operations worldwide with annual net revenues approaching $215 billion. But lately its profitability had foundered on both the disastrous world oil debacle, post the Israeli-Iranian nuclear holocaust, and the ongoing, aggressive actions of the Russians to corner the world's oil market. In addition, Global, and many of its brethren companies, were almost always under continuous investigation by the SEC and the DOJ for alleged price rigging, consumer gouging, Climate Change disinformation and monopolistic antitrust practices generally. So Chairman Kelly was quite apprehensive when he received the unexpected urgent summons to meet with Secretary Finlay.

"Please come with me, sir, the Secretary is anxious to speak with you." Finlay's secretary said. As she opened a large wood-paneled door Secretary Finlay rose to greet the Chairman. The Secretary's well-appointed office was on the top floor of the James V. Forrestal

THE VIKING SANDS : ENDGAME

Building on Independence Avenue, SW, with sweeping views over both the National Mall and the Tidal Basin.

"Good to see you again, George," Finlay said. "Thanks for coming on such short notice."

"Sure, Andy, we always heed his master's voice." Kelly replied with a smile. Despite the formality of the situation, Finlay and Kelly were old friends, both having started their divergent careers together in the West Texas oil patch as rank wildcatters.

"Let me begin to explain, George, why we rushed you here. Strange as it may sound, we're going to need some help from Global. I want you to meet several other people who have just arrived. They will fill you in on what we need." With this, on cue, Finlay's secretary ushered in two men, one of whom looked quite familiar to Kelly.

"Let me introduce you, George, to CIA Director, Tim Baker and his right-hand man, Chris Wytham, Director of their Counter-Terrorism Unit. Obviously our discussions today will be both off-the-record and top secret."

"Oh, are we in trouble again, Andy?" Kelly asked hesitantly.

"No more so than usual." Finlay chuckled. "But as a context for the request we will make to you, please tell us first about Global's dealings with the Russians these past few years. It hasn't been easy, we know, but at least you have a foothold there."

Relieved but quite intrigued, Kelly began to explain. "Yes, we have been negotiating with Transneft, Rosneft and the Kremlin for years. They have always held all of the cards. We kept trying to negotiate a Production Sharing Contract with Rosneft for a greenfield oil prospect in western Siberia, near the ice free port of Arkhangelsk, but we were stymied at every turn. The Duma wouldn't nominate the area for development under the PSC Law; Rosneft insisted on retaining a significant majority interest; and the Kremlin kept throwing up other roadblocks. In addition, the State pipeline monopoly,

Transneft, wouldn't guarantee that they had any spare capacity in their transit lines to take our production to port, if we ever were to get that far. So it has been very frustrating!"

"Yes, but you did get your foot in the door. You convinced them to let you be a technical adviser to Transneft under a Service Contract to help them manage the efficient flow of crude oil through the web of field gathering pipelines that converge in Samara and then feed the *Druzhba* exit pipeline to Western Europe, right?" Tim Baker interjected.

"Yes, correct, but it's a lousy deal. We're paid a flat fee in constantly devaluing rubles that doesn't even cover our cost of expatriate staffing. It was the best we could do to gain an initial foothold, but it really isn't commercially attractive."

"Nevertheless, you have a presence there that could be of real help to our national interests." Baker continued. "Chris Wytham here will explain."

"It's quite simple. We would like to second one of our people to your operation. It would be a short-term, very low key/low visibility position. He'd be just another expert amongst your existing crew. We'll pay for all of his costs and expenses, of course." Wytham concluded.

"And what would he be doing with us?" Kelly asked.

"That's classified." Baker replied. "Just let him go quietly about his business for us. He'll be supervised directly from the embassy in Moscow, where Chris will be temporarily posted. But we'll make it well worth your while to accommodate him."

"Oh, how so?"

"Well, DOJ's ongoing antitrust class action suit against the oil industry includes Global. We can make it go away as far as your company is concerned."

"That would be very helpful." Kelly replied. "Tell me more, please."

Discussions continued on for quite awhile before it became time for an early lunch. As hard as Kelly tried to probe deeper, he couldn't get any more information from the group about either the identity or specific duties of their proposed secondee. He would simply have to take it on faith that his company would be serving a vital national interest and that it would be adequately rewarded for it accordingly.

After Kelly left for his return flight to Plano, the remaining group reassembled in Finlay's office. "So who is this secret agent you will be seconding to Global in Russia?" Finlay asked.

Smiling, Baker replied, "You know I can't even tell you that, Andy. But thanks so much for facilitating this meeting and for helping us achieve our objective. These are very treacherous times and the person's identity and specific duties are only available to a very small group of us on a need to know basis."

Back in their unmarked, black Chevy Tahoe returning to Langley, Baker and Wytham continued their conversation. "Is our 'disposable asset' ready yet for deployment, Chris?" Baker asked.

"Very soon, Tim, we are working on him every day. He's anxious to atone."

"But is he still capable of causing additional mass destruction and possible loss of lives?" Baker continued.

"We have him programmed now to do whatever is necessary to serve us, Tim. Although he professes great remorse for everything he has done before, underneath it all he remains fundamentally a sociopath, with no guilty conscience for the consequences of his acts."

"But if he's seconded to Global as a US national it will be a dead give away to the Russians that we are responsible for any of his acts of sabotage. It could escalate fast into very dangerous territory!"

"We thought about that already, Tim. He's of Mizrahi Iraqi Jewish descent, the branch that originated in the Middle East. With some cosmetic surgery and fingerprint wiping he could pass easily for a Chechen or a Dagastani, both of which have been known to perpetrate mass terrorist acts in Russia for decades now. Don't worry, he won't be posted as a US citizen. But he'll be micro-chipped so that we can keep a very close eye on him at all times."

"But where would he have obtained any of the sands? The Russians would blame us immediately."

"Of course they will in any event, but we will have plausible deniability. They believe we have none left. We now know that they certainly don't. We will have no idea where he got the sands, but we would steadfastly maintain that he's not one of ours. Global hires lots of foreign and domestic specialists, so they would profess that any detrimental act by him would be strictly *ultra vires* and rogue. In addition, the Russians are on the verge of launching a brutal war to take Ukraine back into their 'sphere of influence'. Their President is acting very reckless and menacingly toward both NATO and the West. Surely it must be distracting him from his campaign to corner the world's oil markets. So the time for us to strike is definitely now."

"Perfect, Chris! Sounds like you have all of the bases covered. I'll need to review and approve your deployment plan ASAP. By the way, be sure to take Talia Dagani with you to Moscow. She's an excellent analytical expert."

"Of course, Tim!" Wytham replied with a broad smile.

VI

Tuesday, May 21st, CIA Black Site, McLean, VA, 11:30 EDT

Things seemed to be improving for Albert, or so he thought. No more draining, daily interrogations while strapped to a chair, with a glaring light blinding him. Rather, the situation had seamlessly segued to more relaxed conversations about how he could redeem himself by being of service to his country. He had been through so much in such a short time that he was completely cooperative and pliable. The CIA's best brainwashing and mind control techniques had had their desired effect. Sitting in a private room off the black site's cafeteria, he was having a light lunch with Chris Wytham while discussing what the Agency would be expecting of him.

"You will have this one chance, Albert, to rehabilitate yourself. But it won't be easy by any means!"

"I understand, but I'm ready. What must I do further to atone and serve?"

"We need to thoroughly prepare and brief you first. You will be deployed abroad, under cover, reporting directly to me. You will have to undergo some further medical and surgical procedures first, completely to change your identity. You'll be micro-chipped so that we can track your movements regularly. Your new name will be Alik Dudiyn, of Chechen origin, traveling on a Russian internal passport. You need to concentrate hard on your conversational Russian to sound authentic, although your employer will conduct most of its work in English. Before you are deployed you will be given special equipment by our Office of Technical Services to aid you in your assignment. And of course you will be given our only remaining vial of the Viking sands that you will both guard with your life and deploy according to our forthcoming instructions. But if you succeed in your difficult task, you will be fully redeemed and pardoned. We'll have you relocated under the FBI's witness protection program to a new life and identity as an astrophysicist at the National Laboratory in Los Alamos, New Mexico. You will not suffer any severe punishment nor serve any jail time. So do you believe that you are mentally ready now?"

"Of course! How can I thank you for this chance?"

"Simply by succeeding." Wytham concluded.

Before he was returned to lockdown Albert was conducted to the Technical Services Office to receive his special equipment. The Quartermaster there gave him some mini-earbuds that canceled out all ultra high-pitched frequency sounds and several other items that required detailed explanation. Lastly he handed Albert a disassembled, 3-D printed, 9mm caliber Glock 19 handgun clone made of a super-hardened polymer that could neither be detected nor identified by AIT scanners or metal-detectors. He'd receive the assembly instructions and ammunition before he left on his mission.

"Have you ever fired a handgun?" the Quartermaster asked.

"No, sir. Do I really need one?"

"Maybe. Better safe than sorry. So you'll have learn to use it fast. I'll schedule you a tutorial session tomorrow morning at the firing range in the basement."

Back in his bedsitter accommodation, Albert stared long and hard at his new appearance in the mirror. Gone was his long brown hair, substituted by a closely cropped coif. Plastic surgery had given him an aquiline nose, so typical of those of Chechen ethnicity. His fingertips were smooth, having been acid-wiped of fingerprints. His mustache and beard were fully grown out. He looked almost unrecognizable to himself. "Alik Dudiyn, indeed!" he thought. But from then on he would have to get quickly comfortable with being called by his new name and living his new persona.

VII

Monday, May 27th, Helsingin Satama, the Port of Helsinki, Finland, 19:00 GMT +2

Albert had flown directly from Washington to Helsinki-Vantaa

Airport overnight on Finnair. Arriving in the early morning, he had struggled to get the cobwebs of a fitful, sleepless night out of his tired eyes. The day was cold, damp and gray. He had had 12 hours to kill before he could board the Russian-flagged St. Petersburg Line's barebones cruise ship that would take him overnight to the "Venice of the North". As he had been thoroughly briefed to do, he inconspicuously took advantage of an unusual exemption in the otherwise arduous and almost impossible Russian tourist visa process. For only 126 Euros anyone could book a limited 2 night stay in St. Petersburg in sparse accommodations. Included in the package was a shuttle ticket which acted as a temporary "visa" for entry into the city. The shuttle was supposed to provide a supervised tour, but it basically just dumped everyone off in the middle of town and expected them to meet it at the same rendezvous point 3 days later for return to the cruise ship.

Albert had entered Finland on the first of his CIA-crafted passports as Marcel Levine, a French *négociant* from Dijon in the wine export business. It had served him equally well in boarding the cruise ship without any questions being asked. Early the next morning he would arrive unnoticed in St. Petersburg.

VIII

On the 30 minute shuttle ride the morning of the day after from the Marine Facade Port of St. Petersburg into the city center the humorless driver had turned on a welcoming tape which played in a continuous and annoying loop in Russian, English, French and Finnish. In each case it warned occupants that they must return to the drop-off point exactly 3 days later or risk very serious consequences. As Albert disembarked the shuttle at the junction of Nevsky Prospekt and Ligovsky Prospekt he saw the facade of the great

Moskovsky railway station across from him in Vosstaniya Square. He perfunctorily acknowledged the driver's final warning to be back in time, but that was certainly not what he had in mind to do.

Moskovsky Vokzal station is St. Petersburg's oldest and busiest in terms of passenger traffic. Trains from it run mostly between St. Petersburg and Moscow, including their high-speed *Sapsans*, which makes the 633 km journey in just 3 1/2 hours. Albert entered and headed for the ticket office where he bought a one-way Economy Class seat to Moscow for cash. No need to show any identity papers. He had already begun his transformation from French tourist to Chechen-born Russian citizen, Alik Dudiyn.

Later in the week it came to the attention of the St. Petersburg Police that French tourist, Marcel Levine, had failed to turn up at the appointed rendezvous point for return to the cruise ship back to Helsinki. The Police Chief was not at all surprised. While St. Petersburg is a reasonably safe city, there still were gangs of pickpockets and muggers who regularly preyed on foreign tourists, sometimes with fatal consequences.

"Another stupid tourist missing." he dryly observed to his desk sergeant. "Probably mugged while trying to exchange some of his euros for rubles at the black market street rate. Notify our river patrol to be on the lookout for yet another bloated corpse to pop up in the Neva." he continued disinterestedly.

IX

Tuesday, May 28th, Leningradsky Vokzal railway station, Moscow, Russia 13:30 GMT +3

Entering the station's main concourse from the *Sapsans*' dedicated

THE VIKING SANDS : ENDGAME

arrival platform, Albert - *now Alik* - scanned the placards of the crowd of chauffeurs waiting to greet the arriving passengers. Quickly he saw what he was looking for. A large, very American-looking man was holding up a placard headed "Global Oil" with the name Alik Dudiyan penned below it in big block letters. Albert walked straight over to him.

"Mr Dudiyan?" the man asked. "Hi, I'm Bubba with Global Oil Russia Ltd. Let me take your bag. Our vehicle is waiting outside to take you on to Sheremetyevo International Airport to catch the chartered flight later today to Samara. The schedule is a bit tight, but morning traffic has begun to subside. We should make it there easily, with time to spare."

Albert groaned softly to himself. The last thing he wanted to do was to travel any further after almost 3 arduous days of being continuously on the road with very little sleep. What he desperately needed was rest, refreshment and something to eat! So on the way out heading towards the VIP parking lot, Bubba stopped at a street kiosk to get two piping hot black coffees and a selection of delicious Russian pastries - Vatrushka, straight out of the oven, filled with sweetened farmer cheese and some semi-sweet, cylinder-shaped Kulich breads with their small domes topped with sprinkles.

"There's our company truck." Bubba said, pointing to a huge, black GMC Sierra 2500 AT4 pickup with a large wooden crate tightly secured in its flatbed. Albert was much too tired to notice or care though, as he woofed down the welcome food and coffee. His eyes were growing increasingly heavy. All he knew was that he was heading for a direct flight to his final destination at Global's headquarters in Samara, one of Russia's largest industrial cities and the center of a vast confluence of crude oil feeder pipelines.

"So you are a SCADA telemetry expert?" Bubba ventured, while deftly weaving his way through the always chaotic Moscow traffic.

But Albert had already fallen into a deep, satisfying sleep.

X

Wednesday, May 29th, Hotel Baltschug Kempinski, Moscow, Russia 09:00 GMT +3

Chris Wytham and Talia Dagani had arrived in Moscow late on the evening before and checked in as husband and wife tourists from San Pedro, California, under assumed names. Waking up cuddled together to the glory of an unusually bright spring morning, Talia was dazzled by the almost heavenly glow of the sun glistening off the golden domes of the Kremlin's cathedrals across the Moskva River. It was a surreal sight that she had never expected ever to see.

"Oh Chris," she purred in his ear, "have you ever seen anything so beautiful and serene?"

"No, Talia darling, never before." Chris lied. Earlier he had been CIA Chief of Station at the embassy in Moscow for over 5 years. "Cathedral Square is such a beautiful sight, but I have something far more beautiful here with me now." he continued, looking deeply into Talia's limpid, dark brown eyes. He was in the mood for some 'morning delight', but as always, duty called. He whispered a caution into Talia's ear about refraining from any "shop talk", indicating that the chances of their room being bugged was almost 100%.

Getting reluctantly out of bed, Chris put the electric kettle on to make them both an early morning cup of Russian caravansary tea. He picked up his burner cell phone and tapped in a secure code. It immediately put him in touch with the nearest US Orion NROL-44 intelligence satellite orbiting Earth at a distance of about 36,000 km. These surveillance satellites "hoover up" hundreds of thousands of cell phone calls; scour the dark web for terrorist activity; and mingle with commercial telecommunications satellites and the worldwide GPS network. The latter was the interface that Chris wanted to reach. A quick, encrypted download from the satellite gave him a read-out of all of Albert's movements that had been recorded by his microchip since he left DC.

"It looks like our friend has arrived, dear. Did you book him in too for the city tour we are going to take this morning? We are supposed to meet him in front of the Red Square bus stop at 10:00. It should be a really exciting day!" Chris improvised.

With that they hastily packed up their light suitcases, checked out and hopped into an unmarked Volga GAZ 24 sedan waiting outside to take them to the US embassy.

XI

Wednesday, May 29th, Global Oil Operations Center, Samara, Russia 07:00 GMT +4

Albert would have to get quickly used to his new role and identity as Alik Dudiyn, SCADA telemetry expert. It would take at least a week for him to familiarize himself with the layout and operation of Transneft's vast pipeline hub at Samara. Major production flows of crude oil converge there from Russia's most prolific oil producing regions in Western Siberia, Timan-Pechora, the Urals, Volga and from the Caspian Sea basins in the "near abroad", before being transferred into the *Druzhba* ("Friendship") Pipeline for export to Western Europe. At full capacity *Druzhba's* 36" pipeline could transport up to 2 million bbls/day. But it wasn't the export section that would be Albert's target. It was the upstream feeder sources from where the crude oil was produced and collected.

Up early after a long night's sleep, Albert headed for a hearty breakfast in the cafeteria. It was already crowded with both Global and Transneft workers. As he looked for a table a towheaded giant of a man gestured for Albert to join him.

"Hi, Alik, is it? I'm Lucus Cole, Global's Crew Chief. The men call me "Big Luke". Welcome to our operations center."

"Thanks. Nice to meet you."

"We hold a meeting every morning at 8:00 where I brief the men on the day's operational schedule and hand out their assignments. It will be over in the assembly hall. Do you know where that is?"

"Yes Big Luke, I do. I'll be there."

"Good. Just a private word first, though, about staff interaction. You know that we are here to assist Transneft in scheduling and operating the web of feeder pipelines that bring crude from all over to this hub. It's fairly obvious that Transneft didn't really think that our assistance was necessary. So their people tend to be pretty standoffish. They keep to themselves and they don't mingle at all with us socially. But don't be put off by that. They do their jobs well. Just be very careful how much you tell any of them about yourself. We know that their ranks have numerous FSB agents embedded in them to keep an eye on us. So keep it very professional, OK?"

"Got it. I suppose that's to be expected."

"We all have a negotiated form of 'diplomatic immunity' that prevents us from being prosecuted for alleged spying and such, but we never want to test it. They can bounce any of us out of here in 24 hours flat if accused. Better than going to the *gulags*, though, I guess!" Cole said with a wry smile.

"Thanks for the heads up." Albert replied. As Cole left Albert lingered to finish his second cup of coffee then and headed over to the meeting hall to receive his first assignment.

XII

Before crude oil can be sent through a pipeline for export it needs to be initially treated to remove contaminants such as sulfur, thiol mercaptans, nitrogen, ground water and heavy metals. The treating process, primarily hydrotreating, removes these chemicals by binding them with hydrogen, absorbing them in separate columns, or adding acids. The end result of such treatments at Samara is the production of pipeline quality 31.7 API gravity Urals Blend, which is a mixture of heavy, sour Urals crude and Volga Region light oil from Western Siberia. It's the reference oil blend used as the basis for pricing of Russian export oil mixtures supplied through the *Druzhba* pipeline to Western Europe and to the southern Mediterranean region. Urals blend accounts for more than 80% of Russia's oil exports and for its vital hard currency earnings.

The key for Albert's task would be to learn the daily and weekly shipment schedules of crude oil coming in from the various feeder pipelines originating at the prolific cluster of oilfields supplying it.

As he began to familiarize himself with the workings of the massive complex, he heard a voice from behind him greet him in Chechen.

"*Jüyre dika yoyla.*" the voice said. Albert had learned just enough Chechen to understand that much.

"*Dobre outre, vi govorite po-angliyski?*" he responded in Russian.

"Of course I speak English, but I thought that you were Chechen?"

"Of Chechen descent, but I've been a long time away."

"Anyway, I'm Akhmad Islamov, an engineer with Transneft. You are Alik? Glad to make your acquaintance!"

"Yes, thanks, the same."

"Where was your family from in Chechnya?" Akhmad asked.

Remembering what Big Luke had told him about FSB agents being embedded in Transneft, Albert was reluctant to get into any detail of his background. It was enough just to say "The outskirts of Grozny."

Akhmad obviously wanted to probe deeper into Albert's background and this immediately set off alarm bells. He decided quickly to shift the conversation to only technical matters. "So how often do shipments come in from each feeder line for processing here?" he asked.

"Oh, there's an intricate schedule posted every day. Do you know where to look?"

"I'm sure I'll find it. What are your duties this morning?" Albert asked, noting that Akhmad was carrying an expensive, weatherproof SONY Alpha 7C digital camera equipped with a sophisticated, high-resolution lens package.

"We have just done some ultrasonic scans on the feeder pipelines' flanges that connect to the main 36" pipe going into the treatment plant. There appears to be some possible corrosion and cracks. I'm here to take some photos to confirm their locations."

"Oh, weren't the scans enough to do that?"

"I'm just supposed to verify their findings. Here, could you help me out, please? Let me snap a few photos with you in the foreground to calibrate my field and give the photos a sense of scale."

Albert wasn't keen, but he could hardly refuse. It seemed like a harmless request. Reluctantly he stood where Akhmad asked him to as the latter snapped away in rapid succession. Then he took his leave as Akhmad appeared to get on with his appointed task.

PART 9
ENDGAME

"Time wounds all heels and then heals all wounds."

I

Wednesday, May 29th, Rublyovka District, Western Suburbs of Moscow, Russia, 09:00 GMT +3

The vastly wealthy Russian Oligarchs were getting increasingly nervous. They had tacitly gone along with the President's attempts at world economic domination by him successfully playing the oil trump card. But now they were totally unnerved by his sudden decision, in tandem, to seek to expand the borders of the Russian Federation by initiating a brutal and unprovoked military invasion of their largest neighbor to the west. It smacked of irrational behavior and it was already hurting them badly economically. While the President's patronage over the years had helped them build huge stores of wealth, his current, unrestrained course of action was heavily damaging their lucrative business empires. They had tried to warn him off carrying out his proposed "Special Military Action", but alone and isolated with his loyal, conservative *siloviki* - the former KGB security men who surrounded him - the President had dismissed the Oligarch's protestations as both irrelevant and bordering on being seditious. Something had to be done about the President's recklessness fast. While it wasn't strictly a personal matter, it was most definitely an urgent business one!

In response, Alexander Potanin, Chairman of *Rossiya Kommersiya*

Bank, had decided to convene a highly secret meeting of his Oligarch peers to discuss the damaging behavior of the increasingly isolated and paranoid President. He waited anxiously to greet them at the door of his sumptuous mansion in the richest of Moscow suburbs as they arrived in a convoy of luxury vehicles.

"*Privyet!*" he saluted each of them as they filed into his lavish main sitting room.

"*Slava*," he addressed one of his peers, "the President's unpredictable behavior is ruining us! Sanctions on him are perhaps understandable, but now we too are to be caught in their ever-expanding net."

"Indeed, *Sasha*, we will become hunted men. I can't sell or hide my assets fast enough to avoid them being frozen or confiscated. He has gone much too far to enrage the united NATO alliance against us. The very continued existence of our country could be at stake if he isn't immediately stopped. He must either be forced to step down or be removed in a coup."

"Perhaps", another of the Oligarchs ventured, "the military or the FSB can do the dirty work for us? Old Volkov would never have turned against his long-standing patron, but what do we know of the sympathies of his young successor, Kalashnik? If his armies don't swiftly and completely succeed against the Ukrainians he could not feel too secure in his new position. And then there's the new man, Luzhkov, at the FSB. Where does he stand?"

"We know very little of either of them," Potanin replied, "but I doubt that Kalashnik has the standing with the General Staff yet to engineer such a coup, even if he was willing to do so. Nor do I have any hope for support from the FSB. Luzhkov is a Chestnoy protégé, totally loyal to the current regime."

"So we have no viable options, *Sasha?*" the disconsolate Oligarch lamented.

"Perhaps we still do. I have been clandestinely in touch with Ibragim Dimaev, the radical and uncompromising leader of the Chechen Separatist Movement. They still have a deep, smoldering hatred for the President after he ordered the complete destruction of their capital city, Grozny, some 20 years ago. They have been spoiling to take revenge against him ever since."

"Is Dimaev willing, then, to carry out an assassination? At what price to us, though? If he fails we are all dead men!"

"I know, but these are desperate times and we must be willing to take extraordinary risks. I have told him that we cannot guarantee anything, but that we would certainly support a large measure of devolved independence for Chechnya under a new, democratically-oriented regime in Moscow."

"And how and when could he carry out such an operation without exposing us?" another of the Oligarchs wondered worriedly out loud.

"I have left it to him to decide on the appropriate time and means, but he knows that it must be very soon. He and his operatives are very skilled in succeeding with acts of terrorism."

"So the deal is sealed, then?" *Slava* asked.

"If you all now agree, *konechno*, it would be."

"*Saglasna*", the assembled group nodded in complete accord.

II

Friday, May 31st, Tomb of the Unknown Soldier, Alexandrovsky Gardens, Moscow, Russia, 09:00 GMT +3

The Tomb of the Unknown Soldier is located in the Alexandrovsky Gardens, outside the Kremlin wall, on the northwest side of Red Square. On the crimson marble mausoleum facing north and east/west, bronze sculptures of steel helmets and military flags are displayed. A convex five-star torch in front of the Tomb has an Eternal Flame that has been burning continuously since it was first kindled in 1967. The Kremlin Regiment, also called the Presidential Regiment, is the military unit that maintains a constant Guard of Honor at the Tomb.

The Commandant of the Guard had just finished morning roll call when he was quite surprised to see workmen arriving. It seemed that they intended to place sawhorses and "construction site" yellow tape streamers around the area of the polished, red porphyry granite pavers located directly in front of the Tomb and the Eternal Flame.

"Halt!" he ordered them brusquely. "What do you think that you are doing? This is sacred ground!" He was especially disgusted to see that the entire work crew consisted of Central Asians.

Unfazed, the crew's foreman drew a document out of his overalls to show to the Commandant. "Just following orders, *tovaritch*. We are here to do repointing and re-grouting of the pavers in this area. They have become loose due to constant freezing and thawing over the years. We will do no damage and complete the work as fast as we can."

Skeptically the Commandant studied the work order. It looked official. It bore the seal of the Federal Protective Service, the government department charged with ensuring the security of the Kremlin and its treasures. He knew that the President was due to come in a week's time to lay a wreath at the Tomb to honor the many Russian soldiers who had already been lost in prosecuting the current Special Military Action to "liberate" Ukraine. So it all had better be in absolute perfect condition for him, he reasoned.

"Get on with it then. Do it as quickly as possible. We will next change the Guard at 10:00 and you must not be here to interfere."

The workmen carefully chiseled out the old grout and lifted the highly polished stones up from their placements. They laid what the

Commandant assumed to be new waterproof insulation underneath them. It was a thick, opaque, plastic material, secretly containing an invisible web of circuit wires in each sheet. The crew then grouted the pavers firmly back into place and completed a hasty cleanup and polishing of the stones. In almost an hour's time the workmen were gone as quickly as they had come.

III

Tuesday, June 4th, Ongudaysky District of the Altai Republic, Siberia, Russia 11:00 GMT +6

The President was hidden safely away in his purpose-built underground bunker complex in the Altai mountain region of Siberia. But he was in a very foul mood this morning. His military campaign in the Ukraine wasn't going according to plan. It was supposed to have been a lightning-fast conquest that would send a stern warning to NATO. Instead his forces were bogged down on several fronts, encountering fierce resistance from both the Ukrainian military and the country's Civilian Militia defenders. Many Russian soldiers had already been lost, along with large numbers of armored and supply vehicles, artillery pieces, attack helicopters and jet fighter-bombers. The President was angry, isolated and increasingly paranoid. His actions had become both desperate and unpredictable. He knew it was a war he couldn't afford to lose. So he wanted some answers fast.

"Get me Lieutenant General Kalashnik immediately." he commanded. Moments later the General was on a secure line to him from his forward command position in Voronezh.

"What the hell is the delay? Why haven't you taken Kyiv yet?" the President demanded.

"We are quite near now, *Gospodin President*. We have it completely encircled. I am confident that it will fall within the next few days."

"Not good enough!" the President raged. "Bomb and shell them into submission. Use all weapons in our arsenal, including chemical, biological and even tactical nuclear, if necessary. That's what Volkov would have done. Don't make me regret having appointed you Chief of the General Staff." the President menacingly concluded.

IV

Tuesday, June 4th, The Lubyanka, Moscow, Russia, 09:00, GMT + 3

New FSB chief Lieutenant General Mikhail Luzhkov was startled to read the report he had just received from the OTU, his Technical Operations Directorate. With tensions running very high between Moscow and Washington, surveillance at Global had been ratcheted up to the highest level. Akhmad Islamov, a FSB lieutenant embedded with Transneft in Samara, had sent the pictures he had snapped of Alik Dudiyn on to the FSB's Facial Recognition Unit for analysis as standard procedure for any new 'person of interest'. Numerous things about this latest Global employee just hadn't rung true to Islamov.

FRT, or Facial Recognition Technology, is a biometric software application capable of uniquely identifying or verifying a person by comparing and analyzing patterns based on the person's facial contours. Simply put, everyone has a unique facial structure. The state-of-the-art FRTechLabs software that the FSB used was able to analyze one's features; match them with information in a database; and identify who the person is.

A photo of a face is captured and analyzed. Distinguishable landmarks or nodal points make up each face. Each human face has 80 nodal points. Facial recognition software will analyze the nodal points, such as the distance between eyes or the shape of cheekbones. The analysis of a face is then turned into a mathematical formula. These facial features become numbers in a code, called a "faceprint". Similar to the unique structure of a thumbprint, every person has their own faceprint. The code is then compared against the main database stored in the Integrated Center for Data Processing and Storage in Moscow that has photos that can be compared to make an identification.

Lukhzov couldn't believe what he was reading. The FRT analysis that had been done plainly concluded that despite cosmetic and surgical changes to his facial features, the pictures of "Alik Dudiyn" that Islamov had sent to be analyzed were clearly those of Albert Stern.

"Pavel, " he ordered his adjunct, "get Borisenko on the line immediately!"

"Colonel", Lukhzov said to Borisenko, "I have an urgent job for you and Major Fortunatov. It's some pressing 'wet work'." He then went on to detail the circumstances of Albert Stern being inexplicably present at the Transneft compound in Samara. "Truly unbelievable and very dangerous! We have all had enough of this persistent nuisance. We don't know what he's up to but it couldn't be any good for our national security. It's time for him to expire once and for all. You two go there immediately and kill him. No mistakes! I want him dead. You have my full authority to carry out this task with impunity, understood?"

"Of course, General. I have been looking forward to closing out this sordid affair for the longest time." Borisenko replied with relish.

V

Thursday, June 6th, US Embassy, Bolshoy Deviatinsky Pereulok No. 8, Moscow, Russia GMT +3

Chris Wytham was intently engaged on his laptop. He was logged in as "Hawk" and connected on a secure satellite link to "Cardinal", Albert's code name in Samara. The time had come to give him his final instructions:

Hawk (H): Report fill status of feeder pipelines.

Cardinal (C): All completely full with backups to every producing region. No processing being carried out due to embargo on shipments through the *Druzhba*.

H: Good. What day(s) are maintenance operations carried out on the main 36" feeder line into the processing plant?

C: Every Friday morning for several hours. I have now gotten to know the routines and the hardware configuration very well.

H: Then the time has come for you to carry out your orders. It must be tomorrow.

C: I'm ready. How do I introduce the vial of sands into the pipeline system?

H: Remember the rough diagrams that we showed you before you left? The vial of sands must get into the section of the main 36" pipeline at its interface with the feeder lines. At the junction where those numerous lines join the main pipeline there is a hydraulically operated trap door on top that allows full access to the joint section for inspection and maintenance when empty. It allows the steel rams and dual ball valves that seal off flow into the processing plant to be inspected until they are manually opened. It's a simple operation to turn the opening wheel above the valves and commence the flow of oil. Stay far away from the opening after you've thrown the vial in, though, as the crude will surge forward under immense pressure!

C: Yes, OK. I've studied the layout carefully and I see now how it can be done.

H: Be sure that the noise-canceling buds are firmly placed in both of your ears before you begin. Also have your handgun ready for any unforeseen eventualities. Keep me fully informed of your progress and results. We shall be tracking you minute-by-minute on GPS. You must not fail!

As Wytham signed off Talia entered the room. "Did he understand all of his final instructions, Chris?" she asked.

"We can only hope so, Talia."

"Does he seem to appreciate the immense danger that he will be in?"

"Probably. He has seen what the sands can do. I think he knows that his chances of survival are slim. If both the immense heat and aura generated doesn't kill him the ensuing shock wave most probably will. But he's both a fatalist and a gambler and he knows that he has nothing to lose, but everything to gain if he succeeds."

VI

Friday, June 7th, Global Oil Operations Center, Samara, Russia 13:00 GMT +4

Alik Dudiyan appeared to his colleagues to be busy scanning telemetry readouts from the newly upgraded SCADA system. They showed the degree of fill/ullage and the status of movements of batches of crude oil through the feeder pipelines into the vast hub at Samara. Due to the growing embargo on Russian oil, the pipelines were filling up with volumes of crude that could be tracked all the way back to their sources in the various producing regions. The system was quickly approaching overload with no significant outflows. Suddenly a veritable glut of crude oil had accumulated with no market into which to send it. This was certainly contrary to the President's plan for world oil market domination and another source of worry to those who would suffer his wrath if it failed.

Every week the large feeder flange into the crude oil processing plant was sealed off for routine cleaning and maintenance. No new oil could flow through it during these times. Everything remained backed-up until the necessary procedures had been completed.

As Alik continued his monitoring a forklift appeared with the large wooden crate he had seen through sleepy eyes in the back of the truck that had picked him up from Moscow. It was unloaded and opened, revealing what looked like some additional telemetry equipment that had been shipped from the original supplier in Lingren. Albert didn't know why, but he had been told to put the mini-earbuds that canceled out all ultra-high frequency sounds into his ears once the new piece of machinery was ready to operate near to the SCADA control system. He did so, feeling uneasy that he also had the fully assembled Glock 19, loaded with a standard 15 bullet magazine, uncomfortably tucked away in his cargo pants pocket.

The new machinery started up and unexpectedly began to emit an ultra high-pitched frequency sound that was immediately unbearable. It was exactly what victims of the "Havana Syndrome" had often reported. And indeed, that's what sort of noise this disguised directed energy weapon was generating. It swiftly blanketed the area with ear-piercing sounds for 100 meters around, rapidly causing disabling symptoms of headache, nausea, hearing loss and vertigo to all within reach who heard them.

VII

The ultra fast Mi-24 military helicopter carrying Borisenko and Fortunatov from Moscow touched down at the Transneft/Global helipad at 13:15 Samara time. When they were greeted there by Big Luke, Borisenko just asked him brusquely where they could find Alik Dudiyan.

Miffed, Big Luke replied "Over by the main pipeline junction monitoring telemetry readouts of crude oil about to be moved into the processing plant after all inspections are completed. That's his job here."

"What's that high pitched noise? It's terrible!" Borisenko exclaimed. Neither he nor Fortunatov were carrying noise-canceling headphones.

"We don't know," Big Luke replied, "but we're working on shutting it down."

Unfazed, the two FSB operatives pushed past Big Luke and headed straight for where their quarry was carrying out his own mission. His Glock 17 service revolver drawn, Borisenko approached the unsuspecting figure from behind.

"So we finally meet, Stern." Borisenko shouted above the ear-piercing noise. "I have been waiting for this moment for a long time!"

But Borisenko was surprised to see what Dudiyan was doing as the latter whirled around to face his assailant. Perched on top of the pipeline junction with the access trap door open in front of him, he was about to throw something into the empty cavity. He had his other hand on the wheel that would open the flow of crude oil into the system. The deafening noise was already causing serious vertigo for both Borisenko and Fortunatov as each of them tried to level their gun to take a clear shot.

Dudiyan knew that he was in an untenable and exposed position. His only hope was to kill before being killed. The noise-canceling earbuds were working well as he drew out his handgun and pointed it at Borisenko in the foreground. He fired off a rapid succession of rounds, but his aim was less than perfect. His bullets ricocheted wildly off the heavy metal pipeline infrastructure surrounding the three of them. Both of the FSB agents were seriously injured in the errant barrage. Neither of them would likely survive their wounds. But in the confusion and melee Dudiyan had taken a shot to his chest from Fortunatov, who was standing just behind Borisenko.

Dudiyan slumped down over the control wheel, fatally wounded. Summoning his last bit of rapidly waning strength he struggled to open it to full. His balance gone, he slid perilously closer to the yawning opening in the pipeline junction in front of him. Still clutching the vial of Viking sands, he found himself unable to keep his footing. With a dying gasp he tumbled head first into the rapidly filling void. As he disappeared beneath the searingly hot, highly pressured flow of crude oil that engulfed him, the hydraulic trap door slammed shut over him.

The ensuing reaction was instantaneous and catastrophic. An immense, telltale blue-white aura erupted high into the sky and began to engulf the entire pipeline hub. Crackling with searing heat and static electricity, a monstrous tempest rolled out from the junction point of the pipeline hub preceded by an ear-splitting crash and a massive high-speed shock wave. The Viking sands were doing their final destructive job. Methodically they were proceeding up the feeder pipelines towards the very heart of Russia's massive Western Siberian oil reserves. In a matter of minutes they would entirely consume most of the 80+ billion barrels of crude oil reserves that were the central core of Russia's wealth and power. In just a few moments, the President's dream of global economic domination and restoration of Russian glory through hegemony over the world's oil resources would be gone forever.

VIII

Thursday, June 6th, US Embassy, Bolshoy Deviatinsky Pereulok No. 8, Moscow, Russia, 12:15 GMT +3

Wytham and Dagani had been monitoring Alik's location, movements and vital signs intently through streaming readouts from his implanted microchip. They had pinpointed him by GPS at the junction flange where he was to introduce the sands into the pipeline system. Everything seemed normal until suddenly, at 12:25, his blood pressure began to spike and his heartbeat soared. Something critical was happening. His vital signs continued to fluctuate wildly for several minutes and then dropped abruptly to flatline. No end of attempts to refresh them succeeded.

"He's gone Talia, but did he succeed?" Wytham asked anxiously.

Before Dagani could offer her conjecture, though, they were both distracted by a sudden news flash on Rossiya 1, the primary State-owned TV news channel:

"We interrupt our regular programming to report news just coming in of a major explosion at the Transneft oil pipeline hub in Samara. Full details are as yet unclear, but we can confirm that it caused both considerable loss of life and catastrophic damage to property. Preliminary reports are that this could have been an act of sabotage by a Chechen terrorist. We will keep you informed as additional information is obtained."

"It sounds like he achieved total success, Chris."

"And so ends the life of a tormented soul. Albert did all we could have asked of him. Maybe it was the only way that he thought he could redeem himself. I never would have imagined him as a hero, but he'll be recognized for having destroyed Russia's power. We might be living in a very different and better world tomorrow, thanks to Albert. In any event, our work is done here, Talia. Time to go home."

IX

Friday, June 7th, Tomb of the Unknown Soldier, Alexandrovsky Gardens, Moscow, Russia, 13:00 GMT +3

The atmosphere in central Moscow was tense as the President arrived for the wreath laying ceremony at the Tomb of the Unknown Soldier. Large, angry crowds had gathered to protest just outside the Gardens, in nearby Manezh Square. They were vehemently opposed to the President and his war. Many of them were supporters of the populist, anti-corruption reformer, Anatoly Navrozov, whom the President had ordered to be imprisoned indefinitely on numerous trumped-up charges. But the crowds had been kept brutally at bay by large squads of Moscow Police in riot gear, supplemented by a platoon of lethally armed members of the President's own Presidential Security Service.

After a thorough security sweep, the President stepped out of his heavily armored Zil limousine to the strains of the Hymn of the Russian Federation. He walked confidently towards the ornate wrought iron frame in front of the Eternal Flame, upon which his tributary wreath would be solemnly laid. As the Guards dutifully saluted him a disturbance from behind momentarily caught his attention. The most senior member of his *siloviki* was desperately trying to catch up to him. Pushing his way through the startled Guards he blurted, "*Gospodin President*, we have just had the most catastrophic news from the FSB in Samara! There has been an explosion...."

THE VIKING SANDS : ENDGAME

"Shut up, you fool!" the President icily rebuked him before the man could finish his sentence. "How dare you interrupt this solemn ceremony? Remove him immediately!" the President ordered the startled Guards.

Just outside the fence enclosing the Gardens a nondescript Chechen man looked down at his cell phone for a reply to the text that he had just sent to Dimaev confirming that the President was in position in front of the Tomb. Upon receipt of a coded answer and with a laconic smile, he sent a lethal electronic command.

With his head slightly bowed in reverence, the President was assisted by two of the Kremlin Regiment Guards to place the huge wreath of red roses on the frame. But in the midst of the ensuing moment of silence a huge blast erupted from under the pavers in front of the Tomb, completely enveloping the President and his two unfortunate Guards. In a moment they were all blown to pieces, leaving nothing but a smattering of blood and guts. The ruinous 20+ year reign of the greatest Russian villain since Joseph Stalin had just ended in a fittingly barbaric way.

EPILOGUE

Six months later on Monday, December 9th, at CIA Headquarters, Langley, Virginia, 09:00 EST

"I know of no higher form of patriotism, no clearer expression of what it means to serve with dignity and honor."

There is no more solemn occasion at the CIA than the unveiling of a new star chiseled into the white marble of the Memorial Wall, located just to the right of the main entrance hall. The heading above the Wall bears the simple inscription:
> *"In Honor Of Those Members Of The Central Intelligence Agency Who Gave Their Lives In The Service Of Their Country."*

The Wall would now bear 138 stars carved into the marble; 100 identified as officers who could be revealed; and 38 who would always remain secret, even in death.

A crowd of analysts, caseworkers, administrators and Agency top management had begun to assemble in the space in front of the Wall, completely obscuring underfoot the great CIA seal inlaid in granite on the floor. Amongst them, towards the back of the crowd, were newly engaged Chris and Talia holding hands. As Director Tim Baker approached the podium, the crowd fell silent in anticipation.

"We gather here today to honor one of our own who made the supreme sacrifice in service to his country." Baker began. "The circumstances of his demise are such that his name cannot ever be revealed. Those very few of you who knew him must always keep your sacred oath of silence." he cautioned.

"Our fallen colleague was a tortured soul who made the difficult transition from initial evil to ultimate good. What he did was both heroic and potentially life altering for us all. The world is a safer place now for his sacrifice. He completed his final mission and we are here today to praise and remember him for it. As he amply demonstrated by his selflessness, every new day is a sacred gift that gives us the opportunity to reconstruct ourselves anew out of the salvage of our yesterdays." Baker continued.

"Some of the changes occurring now were inevitable. The horrendous cloud of nuclear fallout that beset the world these last few years has begun to migrate north to the pole, bringing us both new warmth and the first successful harvest back to the northern hemisphere. Our old Cold War enemy, Russia, is just beginning to make a painful but hopeful transition back from complete disarray. Their dictatorial President has been assassinated and, by the overwhelming will of their people, a budding new regime is emerging there under the guidance of those willing to give true democracy yet another chance. Their dastardly plan to hold the world captive by monopolizing its oil resources is forever dashed. Although crude oil availability is still quite scarce and its price remains very high, there has been an unexpected salutary effect of all of this turmoil. Countries desperate to end their over-reliance on oil have turned towards renewable energy sources such as solar and wind power, green hydrogen, and experimental cold fusion to fill their energy gaps. Financial markets are beginning to revive and world liquidity is slowly being restored. The widespread civil unrest that stemmed from the lack of adequate food, warmth and shelter has started to subside. Although the after effects of our colleague's misguided initial deeds were felt worldwide, the 21st century now portends hopeful new prospects for us all after the cataclysmic way it began."

Baker then turned towards the Wall and on his signal, and to a rousing round of applause from all assembled, a small black shroud was lifted off to reveal Albert's anonymous star.

Made in the USA
Monee, IL
10 April 2023